A WASTELAND OF OUTLAWS

G. LaVerne Crowell

Other books by:

G. LaVerne Crowell

ICEX Intelligence, Vietnams Phoenix Program

Mountain Trials

The Roar of War

The Mark of the West

The Mark of the West II

A Crown of Glory

ISBN: 978-0-578-00474-7
Published by Crowell Publishing

DEDICATION

To my lovely wife Joyce
Thanks for putting up with me while I write

CHAPTER ONE

The daylight was slowly seeping off into the coming darkness. Joe was riding along and watching the lonely terrain. He knew he had to set down shortly since a person could be hurt bad or killed after dark riding in this area. Joe had been in this area about six years now as it was his territory to ride patrol. Joe was an Arizona Ranger and was assigned in the southeast area of the territory. Joe was alone much of the time and did not mind this. He had always felt closer to nature and wild critters than to humans. He at least knew what a wild critter would do and when. Joe was looking for a place he liked to settle down for the night. He knew most of the good areas in his territory to set down for a night or more.

He came upon his site while there was barely enough light to see much. He was glad to arrive here and planned on a good night of rest. He stepped down from Jean, his mare, and began pulling the saddle off her. He always cleaned her down from these human effects at night and let her roam if she wished to find some grass or such. She never went very far and he had never hobbled or tied her. Joe felt they had a relationship since she was always there to help him when he needed.

Joe had pulled the saddle off and froze as he heard a buzzing behind him. Jean reared some and let out a part scream. She knew what was there. Joe had frozen, as he knew the snake had to be located before any action could be taken. He did not want to fire his pistol and let anyone or anything know where he was. He looked behind him and saw the snake all coiled and giving its notice that Joe was not welcome here. He slowly moved forward and shortly the snake was satisfied that he was far enough away to not bother it. Jean settled down and Joe let her go on. He moved his bedroll now, as it seemed to be closer to where the snake was proclaiming as his home.

Joe ate some beans from a can and ate some cracker bread. He did not want to start a fire this evening and he was used to eating many things cold by now. He would make a fire in the morning to make coffee over. After he had eaten he spread his bedroll out and hoped he had smoothed the rocks out from under it. He got his rope and made a circle around the bedroll to help keep the snake away. He never had found if this was a good method or not but it always managed to keep him from getting a friend in bed with him. Snakes are not nice to wake up with and when a person is alone this can be hazardous. Joe rolled himself a cigarette and lay back on his bedroll enjoying the beautiful evening. He finally crawled into his bed and drifted toward the clouds.

The morning sun shown its glory into Joe's eyes and he came around to the current world. Birds were chirping him a 'good morning' and Jean was standing about ten feet from him. She looked at him as he opened his eyes and she seemed to know that they would be moving on shortly. Joe gathered some wood and built a small fire to make some coffee. He could handle many things out in the wilds but his love of morning coffee was not one of these items. This

CHAPTER ONE

morning Joe took a couple of pieces of jerky from his saddlebags and put them in a small pan with some water. He would heat this up and it would be softer for his morning meal. He would add beans to this also.

As Joe squatted by his fire and drank coffee he reflected on the coming day. He would arrive in Tombstone this coming night. He really never minded this town regardless of its nasty reputation. He always found things fairly peaceful there and he could also find some distractions from his daily life at the Birdcage Theater. He needed to have the gunsmith there check his pistol. He was getting a few momentary stops when cocking it. He did not want this happening if he was in dire need of fast action. Joe squinted into the western sky and saw some lower clouds forming. It shouldn't rain however and he was sure of a pleasant ride on to Tombstone.

Joe saddled Jean and packed his effects. He was glad the night had been peaceful and was ready to move on. He brushed the camp out a little and then mounted Jean and headed her west. She seemed to know where he was going now and she almost seemed perky about it. Joe was sure animals knew far more than the humans credited them. Jean was almost prancing as she moved out. Joe was looking around as was his normal procedure and he noticed some Indians up on a far rise. There were three of them and they were standing and watching. He was not concerned since they had been peaceful for more than two years. It seemed once the main leaders had been spread out and separated they had no use for contact with white man. Joe smiled to himself that a person would loose any desire about meeting white men after this person had been cheated so much by them.

About ten in the morning Joe observed a small herd of cattle with four riders. He wondered about this since there were very few cattle in this area. Most were wild that had strayed from a past herd and never had been captured. Joe knew the Indians did harvest these lone cattle as they could. He sat on a slight ridge and watched the herd for a time. There were twelve animals here and the four riders almost seemed as if the were directing the cattle along more hidden trails. Now they were moving along in a small gully shielded by rolling knobs. Joe was getting very interested in this group. He decided to ride to the side and move toward them unseen. He headed off to the south and had already placed the area where they were located.

Joe worked along for about two hours and finally figured he was close to the group. He now was using his stealth and planned to reach a high point to observe if this group was still running true to the course he suspected of them. He dismounted close to the top of his observation point and walked up to keep anyone seeing him plain. He arrived toward the top and now squatted down, looking toward the area these men should be in. They were there and still moving as if they had no concerns. Joe quickly made some calculations and figured where he could reach them without their knowing. He walked back to Jean and mounted. He rode to the spot he had picked and waited. Soon the group was coming.

As the group passed his location, he rode out from behind some brush and confronted the men.

"Nice bunch of cattle there. You guys from around here?" Joe asked.

Joe did not miss the surprise and he saw three of the men looking at the last one as if they were wondering what to do.

"Yup, we need to move them toward the railhead by Bisbee. The boss wants them to ship out there back to the east." The 'leader' said.

"What ranch you guys working with?" Joe asked.

Now there was a short pause and no immediate response. The 'leader' finally said "A new homestead about five miles south of here. These cows got missed in the last round up."

"Damn, don't remember any new homesteads there. Must be very new." Joe said. "Wouldn't think a place so new would have a roundup this fast."

Now the situation changed fast. The 'leader' yelled something to the others and it seemed everyone was reaching for leather. Joe was just ahead as he had expected this. He had them covered and they slumped in their saddles.

"You don't give a man much of a chance, Ranger." The 'leader' said.

"Nope, can't afford that. So now if you boys will help out, I need you all dismounted. No fast movements as I would hate to have this pistol to go off."

The four men slowly dismounted.

"You follow instructions good. Just make sure this continues and we will all see the sunset." Joe said. "You, Shorty, grab your rope and get everyone's hands tied up front. Make sure you do a good job."

"Sure." The man answered.

"Now you others drop your gun belts so I don't have to show off and shoot you." Joe added.

The men all unhooked their gun belts and let them drop. The one man began tying the other up. After the three had been tied then Joe went to the fourth man and tied him. He next helped these men on their horses and tied their hands to the saddle. A couple of the men cursed Joe and Joe just smiled. His next move was a real surprise for the four men. He got a smaller rope from his saddlebag and he had hanging noose knots on this rope. The men were a bit concerned now. Joe didn't say anything and just walked to the men one at a time and put their heads into each knot.

After Joe had snared each of the four men with the one rope, he attached this rope to the saddle horn of his mount. The four men were very concerned now. Joe was enjoying all this as he went about his duty. The cattle would just have to stay here and they might become a feast for local Indians. Joe was heading these four to Tombstone now.

"You can't leave us like this. What if a horse suddenly jumps or decides to run?" One man asked.

"I would strongly suggest you be very careful then." Joe said with a smirk. "The nice thing is if one of you tries, you all get the same treatment. You need to remember that as we move along."

The men cursed Joe again and Joe began the movement toward Tombstone. The weather was still good and the clouds to the west had not grown. This sidestep Joe had made really didn't cost much time and he still would get to Tombstone in daylight. The five men rode along and things were very quiet. Joe kept an eye on the four men plus he was watching higher overview areas in case any Indians might be interested in this group.

CHAPTER TWO

The small group rode into Tombstone about five in the afternoon. Joe took his charges directly to the jail in the new courthouse. He turned them over to a deputy there and gave a brief note on charges. He would see the Marshal in the morning about when a court day could be held for them. He retrieved his ropes and thanked the deputy. Joe was feeling good now, as he had always enjoyed Tombstone. It had the rough edges but then most new towns did. The town was holding a population of around 6,000 yet. Most industry was still mining but some of the mines had dwindled out of ore. A few ranches were also spread around the area and the threats of Indian problems were not seen as a problem now.

Joe's next priority was to get some dust cleaned from his throat. He walked to a saloon and stood at the bar. He was known by many people around here and never had many problems in this town. Things had simmered down considerably since the wild reign of the Earps. They had all left town about two years ago and peace was fairly normal in town. Joe would have a couple of drinks and then get a decent meal. His trail cooking never was much to brag about.

"Hi Joe. See you've been up to no good again." The bartender greeted him. "You had a full load with those four you just brought in. The word has been out they are not very nice men."

"Never had much problem with them. Guess I must have scared them a little." Joe smiled.

"Well your known trademark with that hangman's rope usually does the trick I imagine." The bartender said.

Joe had two drinks and then walked back out on the main street. He knew the place to get some good food and he headed that direction. He walked into the café and looked around. A deputy was also eating here and he invited Joe over to his table. This man was a young lawman but had obtained a good reputation already. He was with the Cochise County Sheriff's Office.

"You been out doing no good Joe?" The man asked.

"Can't say either way I guess. Just brought four men in for your jail." Joe told him. "I found them driving a dozen cattle up to the north here. They didn't really have much to say about them being legal."

Joe ordered a good Mexican dinner and relaxed now. He was enjoying watching various people moving along the boardwalk on the street. Tombstone had about every kind of person you could find anywhere. There were a lot more families here now. A couple of years ago the place was mostly men and of course the ladies at the Birdcage Theater.

"Got any new meat at the Birdcage yet?" Joe asked.

"Well I believe there are two new ones there. Haven't had any personal experience however." The deputy said.

"I suppose your lady friend would object to that. The bad part of having a good woman around." Joe laughed.

Joe's meal came and he dug in. There was not much time for talk now. He was going at the food as if he had been without for days. The customers in the café were talking and

CHAPTER TWO

things sounded somewhat like a beehive. Joe sat eating and he finished with a piece of apple pie.

"Always wondered how they get enough apples to make a pie around here." Joe said.

Must be coming in on the train he figured. He stood up and the deputy followed. They walked out to the street and looked around. Things were looking quiet yet and this was a pleasant time of the evening. Most families were home having their suppers. The deputy had to check at the office so the two men split up. Joe was heading down to the Birdcage. He walked in and got a drink at the bar there. He read the poster on the wall about tonight's business and smiled. The event was called a "French Waltz". Joe looked around the area a little and hoped he might see a new girl. The place seemed to be plenty busy as usual. Joe had enjoyed many 'specials' here over the last few years. Even when the town was a rowdy place, the Birdcage still was peaceful and warm to outsiders.

"Hi stud. When did you get in here?" A nice looking gal said as she brushed up beside Joe.

"Hello. You must be new here." Joe said. "Very nice looking."

"Well, lets go upstairs and watch the show." The girl said.

This seemed to Joe as the right thing to do now. He turned and the girl was already going up the steps. This place had been doing enough business that the stairs were worn down in the middle. The girl, Trixi, had her own special booth upstairs. She led Joe there and closed the heavy curtain to give them privacy.

The show was starting now but Joe was not worried about this now. One gal on the stage was letting out some horrible noise. This probably was called singing to some but here no one would notice very much anyway. A few minutes later Joe was still not interested in the show. He walked back downstairs and got another drink at the bar. He was sipping this when a gunshot was heard in the street. Joe ran out to see what was going on. Guns were still outlawed while people were in town.

Two men were standing in the street and cursing each other. Joe yelled at the two to drop their guns. Both acted as if they heard nothing. Joe stepped off the boardwalk here and walked to one of the men. He laid his gun barrel over the man's head. He dropped to the ground. Now Joe told the other man to drop his gun and this instruction was accomplished. By this time the town Marshal came running up.

"Hello Joe." The Marshal said. "I see you are still working. Guess no one was hurt in this anyway."

"Only heard one shot from inside the Birdcage. Guess I made it out fast enough to stop anything more." Joe stated.

"Well I'll have them sleep it off in the jail for the night. If they are still ready to fight in the morning they can ride out of town." The Marshal said.

"Sounds good to me. Guess I'll get a room and stretch out for some needed rest." Joe said. "Don't have to worry about snakes or such in town anyway. See you in the morning."

"Good. Have a good night." The Marshal said.

Joe walked to a hotel and got a room. The Territory paid for hotel rooms and some daily funding for eats. The pay wasn't fantastic at $50 a month, but Joe seldom spent any of it. He was a simple man that didn't require much in luxuries.

Joe planned to spend two days here in Tombstone if he could get a trial for the four men he brought in. After this he would probably head toward Camp Huachuca. This place had been here almost as long as Joe had been. He knew the post Commander, Colonel Jones and liked the guy. He was a spit and polish man but when the chips were down he was the one a person needed on their side. The camp was involved in trying to stop Mexican bandits from coming up to the

CHAPTER TWO

Territory and stealing. They also were involved with what little Indian trouble might be around. There also were some problems with the Mexican government and these seemed to be increasing as the years went on. Joe was hoping that no war would get running here. A war here would be as bad as the Indians attacks from Geronimo in the past.

The next morning Joe rose and cleaned up a bit. He decided to get a haircut and shave from a barber. He would get some breakfast first and then get this done. The day was looking good here and Joe was hoping to get his pistol checked today also. Breakfast in a town was always nice since a person could get eggs and bacon. Eggs were not available out on the trail. Joe had beans and bacon a lot however. Things had to be simple when you were out in the country. Joe got his breakfast and then the barbershop. He next walked down the boardwalk and headed toward the gunsmith. He had good faith in this man as he not only fixed guns but managed to build some very nice pistols.

Joe arrived at the shop and went inside.

"Morning Joe. How are things with you now days?" The gunsmith asked.

"Hi Jack. Things are basically good but I have a small problem with my pistol. It acts like a jam at certain times when you cock it. Don't want to have it get goofy when I really need it." Joe said.

"Well, let me see it. Jack said as he reached for the pistol. He ran it through several cocks and he was seeing what Joe had said. The pistol was basically worn out. Jack could see some rust inside the workings and he knew a Ranger was out in nasty weather at times.

"I think this thing is about ready for the junk pile Joe. I have a nice piece that I just finished here if you want to see it." Jack said as he held a new pistol.

Joe took the pistol and held it. He cocked it and it was smooth as a baby's rear. He snapped the trigger a couple of times and this thing was a masterpiece. It was a .45 caliber pistol and appeared much like the frontier style Colts.

"That is one very fine pistol Jack. You must have honed every piece in it." Joe said.

"Just as I always do Joe." Jack said.

"How many horses would it take to trade for this? I suppose a lot more than I have." Joe said.

"Probably surprise you. I am asking $25 for it but I'll let you have it for $18." Jack said. "I know that is high, but so is the quality."

"Not that bad for a tuned piece like this." Joe said as he tried it in his holster. "Fits fine there also. Guess I will have to take it."

"Good Joe. You won't have problems with this one I know." Jack said.

Joe paid for the new pistol and gave Jack the old one. He probably could make some new parts and resell it. Now Joe wanted to try the new pistol out to get used to it. Every gun had a special way it handled. The time to find out was now not when you really needed it.

Joe walked to the livery and got Jean. He saddled her and then rode off toward a gulch he knew about. He could shoot here and not be heard very far. Joe was almost excited about his new possession. Men like Joe held pistols and such with a high regard. Their lives usually ended up being saved by their weapons. Joe knew the pistol was a very well built one since Jack had made it. Jack told him it took two months for him to get this one made. Of course this was not full time work. Jack would work on building such things during his day at the shop.

CHAPTER THREE

Joe finished checking out his new gun and mounted up to look around the country some. There were more settlers arriving each week. Homesteads were building up fast. Joe figured within another two years this area would be completely settled. He hoped that the crime would go down then also. Several silver mines were still working but most were by a single man and very little equipment. Some miners managed to get a fair living out of their mines but many were more broke than when they started. Ed Schieffelin had discovered silver originally here and he had also named the mine and the town. The story was that a cavalry soldier had told him he would only find his tombstone out here among the various Indians and bandits. Ed had been around for a long time and was fairly well off now. He moved to California last year to enjoy his money.

As Joe rode along he heard some gunshots off to the right. He looked around and then spurred Jean that direction. He soon found the problem. Two men were shooting at each other. They were among some rocks and basically protected. It seemed neither were very good shots. When Joe rode up he yelled for them to stop this nonsense. Now he noticed these were the same two men that had the face off in town last night. Joe had to laugh.

"OK. You two idiots just continue on and I will check back in a week or so and see if the buzzards found you. Good luck with your shoot out and hope you don't run out of ammo very soon." Joe told them.

Joe rode back off and wondered if these two performed this ritual very often. People could really show some odd behavior at times. This was what the west was about. Joe saved these moments of stupidity for his nights when things needed a little cheerful injection. Joe headed back to town now and he needed to see if the trial was going to happen on his schedule. A person could never tell and a lawman sometimes needed to spend weeks waiting for the legal system to finish what they started. Joe arrived back in Tombstone and tied Jean out front of a saloon. He walked in and ordered a beer. The bartender was new and Joe did not know him.

"You just start work here?" Joe asked.

"Yup. Came in on the train last week from Las Vegas, New Mexico. Things were slowing down there so I needed some more excitement in my life. Had always heard Tombstone was an action place." The bartender said.

"Well hope you get your excitement without getting hurt. That can happen around here to bartenders if they don't watch things." Joe told him.

Joe downed a couple of drinks and walked back outside to see if the courthouse had a schedule for his trial. He looked at the bulletin board in the hallway of the courthouse and found the trial was scheduled in two days. This would be fine since he would only be held here an extra day. Joe walked back to the hotel and decided to catch a nap. Nothing seemed to be happening around here right now. He

CHAPTER THREE

left Jean still in front of the saloon as he did many times. He might need her at moments notice.

Joe had been napping about an hour when he was rudely awakened. There was gunfire on the street below. He looked out the hotel window and observed a gunfight on the street near the bank. He guessed a hold up might have been made and so he buckled his gun on and rapidly took the stairs down. He paused just inside the hotel for a minute and he placed the various people involved in his mind. Joe moved around to get toward the side of the fight. The Marshal was involved as was the deputy. Joe managed to get situated to see both sides of the fight. He next drew his new gun and placed a couple of good shots toward the bad guys. This sobered them up fast and now Joe hollered at them to drop their weapons or face his six-gun again. Both of the men dropped their guns and stood up slowly. The lawmen walked up and carted the two off to jail. Joe followed, as he wanted to know what happened. The two men were placed in a cell and the Marshal came back out and sat down.

"Those two are part of a Mexican bandit group and they were planning on robbing the bank here. Guess they didn't understand what kind of lawmen we have here." The Marshal told Joe.

"They just got into the bank when a citizen came to the office and reported he thought a robbery was going on. By the time we got there both men were outside the bank. Ran right into us." The deputy said.

"Well, seems things are in good shape now. No one hurt?" Joe asked.

"Nope. Things very peaceful until they decided they didn't need to be arrested." The Marshal said.

"You need to wire Huachuca about this. They might be interested about Mexican bandits working up here again." Joe told the Marshal. "I'll mention it also when I get over there after my trial."

"Ok. Now seems a good time for a dust washer. You willing?" The Marshal asked Joe.

"Born and delivered ready. Lead the way." Joe replied.

The men walked to a saloon and this time they took a table along a wall. It might be interesting what they heard now. Joe knew the press system working in small towns. Lawmen many times depended on this system to get information out that they wanted spread. The day now seemed to be ready for the lawmen to relax and enjoy. They had been setting at the table about 30 minutes when a voice called out.

"Stand and face me Ranger!"

Joe did not know what this might be about but he slowly looked around as he rose from his chair. A man never wanted to draw his pistol until he knew what was going on. Joe did notice that the other lawmen were sitting still and watching carefully. Joe stood up fully and turned completely toward the voice.

"SAM! You low down snake. Where did you come from?" Joe stated.

A man dressed in a nice suit was standing and looking at Joe. He now walked up to Joe and they shook hands.

"This low down coyote is a very mean man. He deals and plays cards with a strong ambition. He always seems to keep himself through the years." Joe told the other lawmen. "Sit down Sam."

"Thanks. I never have got you to draw without looking." Sam said.

"Probably good for your health that way." Joe stated. "This man is a gambler but not the kind you see in most saloons. He also is as honest as the day is long."

"Well, that's hard to find now days. We generally don't like gamblers here in Tombstone." The Marshal said.

CHAPTER THREE

"Yes, I imagine that since Doc left there haven't been many come around." Sam said. "I hear Doc finally took the big ride up in Colorado. He did have his good points."

The group sat at the table and talked for a couple of hours. Then Joe had to excuse himself since he needed to write up a report for the trial coming. He had left this behind and now it needed to be completed. The Judge here was known as a fair man but he also needed complete information about the man on trial.

Joe walked to the courthouse and filled out a report then he wanted to sit on the boardwalk and watch people for a time. He always liked watching people and he generally learned things that he could use in the future. He wondered if Sam was going to set up here for a time. Tombstone had a reputation for gamblers and there were many shootings centered on card games. The Birdcage had a basement that was used mainly for high dollar card games. There were a couple of private rooms there also in case the gamblers wanted to take a break with a young lady there.

Finally Joe decided to get some supper. He walked to a café at the end of the street and had decided on a good steak for the night. This café also served drinks so it was popular with many people here. When Joe entered the place he saw Sam sitting there also. He must have felt the hunger need to get something. Joe walked to the table and sat down without saying anything to Sam.

"What is your silence about?" Sam asked.

"Nothing. Just need to get some stuffing for my empty belt line." Joe told him.

They sat and ate their meals and talked about normal things. Sam had been up around Iowa and had been doing well at his trade. Unfortunately some of the locals did not care for him after he managed to relieve a few farmers of their pocket money. Such things always were blamed on the gambler and not the player that lost. An odd thing that people always wanted to blame someone else for their goofs.

A WASTELAND OF OUTLAWS

After Sam and Joe had eaten, Joe decided they should go to the Birdcage again this night. Sam had no objections. He might even get into a good game there. He had played many games in the Birdcage and here most people figured anyone who lost money it was at their mistake. Joe figured he might check out other new girls there. Sam told him this addiction was worse than gambling. The two men stood at the bar and had a couple of drinks. The same show was playing here tonight. Joe figured that the place could run the same show for months and most people wouldn't know it. The girls were basically the main attraction here. The few ladies of town had been excited to get a real theater in Tombstone but when they found out what all was going to be there they kicked up a real fuss.

Sam got involved with a card game downstairs so when Joe was finished with his business he walked down to another saloon. He would sit here for a short time and then head for his hotel. He wanted to get some good rest tonight. The trial tomorrow might go fast and he hoped to get on the trail right after that. He had a big area to cover and sitting around doing nothing was boring after a few hours.

The next morning Joe was up and ready for anything. He walked to the courthouse about 9:30 as his case was to be held at ten. Joe liked to sit in on other things just to see how justice was served. Most of the crime in Tombstone was minor. Major things were either ended by gunplay or sent off to Bisbee for a big trial. This was new to Tombstone but when lawyers and judges arrived to bring law here, things changed.

Joe's case was called at 10 and Joe was called to the stand. He gave his testimony about the four men and next the defense attorney had him to question. The defense did not impress Joe very much since he had gone through many trials that were handled much better. In the end the four men were found guilty of rustling and the Judge sentenced them to five years in Yuma. Case closed. The Territory had prison men

CHAPTER THREE

to gather inmates and transport them to Yuma. This made things much nicer for Joe and other Rangers.

A WASTELAND OF OUTLAWS

CHAPTER FOUR

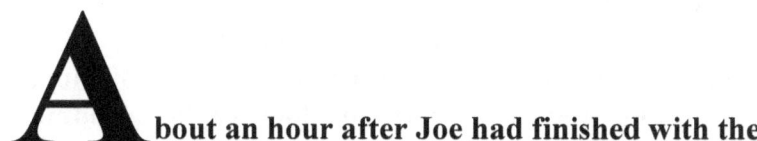bout an hour after Joe had finished with the

trial, he mounted Jean and headed to the west. He was heading toward Camp Huachuca now. He didn't figure to get clear there but he would try to get as far as the San Pedro River. There were times when this river had no water running during the summer but generally a person could dig down a foot or so and get water below ground level. The weather was still nice and that was one thing Joe really liked about his area. Winter got a little cool at times but nothing like northern areas of the Territory. A person would not freeze anyway.

Joe was watching around him as he rode and saw no indication of Indians or other groups. This area was fairly open and therefore most outlaws didn't want to work here. There were a few cattle around at times but generally these were not far from a dwelling. Some of these ranches had been here since Spain had owned the land. Many Spanish Land Grants were still active. The courts usually upheld these grants to ease the exchange of government leadership.

Joe finally saw the afternoon fading. He knew he was only about a mile from the river so he was in good shape. He found a campsite and set up for the night. He took Jeans gear off and set up his bedroll. Now he gathered some wood for a small fire. He planned on a supper of bacon and beans tonight. Tomorrow he could get a good meal from the Army. They always fed lawmen and at no charge to anyone.

Joe placed his rope out again as he knew there were snakes around the place. He ate and sat looking at the fire for a short time. He was getting sleepy so he stretched out on his bedroll. The night was warm so he needed no blanket. It felt good to be out on the range again. He enjoyed his time alone and uniting with nature. He was just another animal out here and he loved it. The night passed easy and the morning came slowly as the sun peeked over the horizon.

Joe opened his eyes and focused for a moment. Next he came full awake as he saw human forms around him. He sat up and looked to see five Indian braves sitting around his camp. He wondered what they wanted. He could speak very little Apache so one of the braves seemed good in English. They wanted to speak with this war chief of the white men. Indians called lawmen war chiefs a lot. It seemed to them to fit these white enforcers.

The Indians knew that Joe had captured the four men with the cattle. These cattle had been ranging with some others close to Indian land and they used them as needed.

CHAPTER FOUR

This was an unwritten law between the Indians and white men. Cattle that strayed off and survived off regular ranches were considered property of the Apache. Joe had always agreed with this. Now these Indian braves wanted to thank the war chief for his help in saving their property.

"Just my job. I work for the rights of people regardless of their race. Those four men were outlaws and would do no good for anyone." Joe smiled.

The brave that was speaking for the others also told Joe he would be watched whenever in their area. They would protect him as they could and this was their sign of appreciation.

"Thank you. I'm sure we will see each other again. I am out around quiet a bit." Joe told them.

The braves now backed off and soon Joe heard pony hoofs as they left the area. This had been unusual to Joe but it was nice to know that not everyone was out to get a person. Joe started a fire again and cooked his breakfast and coffee. He would be arriving in Camp Huachuca this morning. He could see the Huachuca Mountains very plain now.

Joe saddled up and cleaned the camp. He mounted Jean and they were off. Joe was feeling especially good this morning due to the braves in his camp this morning. Joe thought he probably saved the four men's lives also by arresting them. The Indians were not known to forgive white men when it affected them. Joe was happy and he soon rode into Camp Huachuca. He rode to the headquarters and went inside. He met with the duty sergeant and asked about the Colonel. The sergeant excused himself and went to the back. He came back shortly and told Joe to go ahead.

"So how is Colonel Jones this fine day?" Joe asked as he entered the man's office.

"Couldn't be better. Are you working or just goofing off?" The colonel asked.

"You should know. I never work. And from what I've seen lately you haven't been working either." Joe said.

"Well there isn't much trouble with the Indians anymore. Guess I'll have to become a useless Ranger before long." The colonel said.

Joe next told Jones about the Indians this morning. He had never heard of such a thing. They must be impressed by Joe and wanted to show this in some way to him. Colonel Jones stretched and then looked at Joe.

"Any chance of you getting much information about the recent Mexican bandits that has been ranging across the border?" He asked.

"Can't say I heard or seen very much. Were some rumors over in Tombstone however so I figure something is happening. I might ride down that way from here and see what I find." Joe replied.

"That could be very helpful to us." The colonel replied.

The two sat for a few minutes yet in the office and then Joe excused himself to allow the colonel to get back to work. He promised to buy a drink for the colonel later. Joe walked to the post telegraph office and sent a wire to headquarters. This was to let them know he was still around and see if they had anything for him. He advised the operator that he would check back later to see if a return message had arrived.

Joe walked about the camp now and he enjoyed the area. There were larger mountains just to the back of the camp and the temperature never got extremely hot. There was some cold and snow at times during the winter but nothing that could not be handled. Joe sat at the edge of the parade field here and watched a few soldiers as they raked the ground to give it a clean appearance. Military was good at creating work and used it to improve the appearance of areas. The colonel was strong for having formations and parades to show military activity on holidays. At times people would come from a way to see these shows. There was a small settlement just outside the camp but not much for families or loafers in society. The camp had constructed some new barns for the animals here and it appeared as if they were beginning to work toward good housing for the men. There were still a lot of tents scattered around but most of the soldiers did have wooden barracks to stay in.

Around noon Joe walked to the settler's saloon here and had some beer and a few bits of free lunch the man put out. He could sit here and talk with this man and learn what was going on around the place. The man probably knew more of what was happening than about anyone, including the colonel. The bartender managed to tell Joe a lot about local information since he had been here last. They both joked and enjoyed different stories. The saloon was not busy this time of day.

Finally Joe ordered one more beer and then knew he needed to check with the camp blacksmith about shoes for Jean. He knew it had been a few weeks since they had been changed.

"Thanks for the information and I'll be back later." Joe said. "I need to see about the blacksmith shoeing Jean now.

Joe walked out and headed toward the blacksmith. The colonel had been very good about sharing the camps services for civilians that came around. A person could eat in the mess hall also. The food was not the greatest but there was plenty of it. Joe walked into the blacksmith's shop.

"Good day. Any chance of getting Jean shoed or at least checked?" Joe asked.

"Not much of a chance today. I've been backed up with all these horses that just came back from patrol. I tell them not to ride on those canyon rocks but they don't listen. Some day they will do that and then won't have a horse when they need it." The blacksmith said.

Hank, the blacksmith, had been a civilian here before the army came. He had agreed to get enlisted to the army for their use. He was a big man, standing about 6'3" and weighting about 250 pounds. He had coal black hair and a large mustache. He chewed tobacco constantly and Joe had seen him eat with the plug still in his mouth. That takes a different person. Hank did know about everything needed for horses and even was used to treat some that were injured or sick.

"If you ain't leaving real fast, bring Jean over here for the night and I'll try to get on her in the morning." Hank mentioned.

"Sounds good to me. Shouldn't need her for a couple of days. At least I hope this." Joe replied.

Joe put Jean in a stall here and walked back toward the parade ground. A small formation was gathering at the grounds and Joe wondered if this was a patrol moving out or something else. He watched for a short time and then the group moved out toward the north of the camp. There was a shooting range out there. These troops were going to practice shooting. Joe liked to watch these things so he walked that direction. Most cavalry soldiers carried pistols as well as carbine rifles.

Joe arrived at the range and found a place to sit out of the way. The mounted soldiers now were lined up. There were targets placed at various distances from a trail. Soldiers would ride at a run down this trail and fire at various targets as they came up. This was a bit tricky but could be very useful for soldiers on the move. Targets had to be gained by firing from each side of the horse. The cavalry mounts had to be very used to gunfire from their riders. Joe knew what he went through with his own mounts. Jean had been with him for about eight years and she was very stable if he fired. Good horse.

Joe watched as five men ran the course and he was enjoying the show. A field sergeant came up to run next. This man was an older soldier and Joe would have bet money on him for his expertise with this shooting course. The man spurred his mount and galloped along the trail. The sergeant was firing in time from each side of the horse. He was firing from his right hand and would shoot right then point his arm to the left side. Things were going well and the man was doing a good job of hitting the targets. Suddenly however, the man reached over to the left of the horse and the pistol discharged too soon. The horse dropped as it was killed instantly from the sergeant's pistol round.

The sergeant went down with the horse and his leg was caught under the horse. 1200 pounds of dead weight was not easy to move. The other soldiers ran over to help the sergeant and finally got him free from the horse. His leg had been broken however. The leg bone was sticking out from his trouser leg. The sergeant in charge sent a man galloping back to camp to get a wagon for the man. Joe walked to the gathering of the soldiers. The injured man was very upset about shooting his horse. He had been with this horse for five years. It was too late now to save the animal. The sergeant in charge of the event flatly told the man the horse was going to cost him a few bucks from his pay.

Joe walked back toward the camp and met the wagon driving out to get the sergeant. The incident had shown all that a running gunfight was dangerous. A horse was easier to hit than a man in a battle. Many soldiers had been killed after their horses were killed during a battle. There seemed to be no justice with this.

A WASTELAND OF OUTLAWS

CHAPTER FIVE

Joe went to the saloon next and saw that business was much better. Many of local civilians were allowed to come on post and use the facility. This gave the saloon a chance to make some money since the soldiers were not always allowed to partake of any alcohol. The story of the shooting of the horse was spreading already here. This would get some good mileage around before it was worn out.

The bartender now brought Joe a beer and advised him the telegraph runner had been here looking for him. Joe figured there was a return message from headquarters. He was not concerned right now. He would walk over there after he finished his beer. Joe knew none of the customers here and figured they probably were new to the area. It seemed that the west was constantly gathering new people from back east. The ending of most of the Indians troubles had spurred this on. Joe was afraid that his job would be on the increase with all these new people. Good guys weren't the only ones that came here from back east. Most of the eastern outlaws had form new habits for their trade and at times they weren't very good at this. Joe finished his beer and walked to the telegraph office.

"Hello, I sent a runner for you but he couldn't find you. A message from your headquarters." The telegrapher stated as he handed Joe a piece of paper.

"I suppose they have some nasty job lined out for me." Joe smiled.

He opened the paper and read it. 'Please head toward Bisbee as soon as possible. A problem there about Mexican bandits. See Sheriff.'

"Well that seems fairly straight forward. I was going to get Jean shoed here, but guess that will wait." Joe said.

He walked over to the blacksmiths shop.

"Fraid I can't leave Jean here Hank. Got a message to head for Bisbee about some Mexican trouble." Joe told him.

"Hold on a minute if you can." Hank told him.

He walked to the stall where Jean was. He checked the shoes and now told Joe he would change them right now. He could manage this because of the assignment Joe had received. He went right to work and told Joe to get a drink and he would be finished with the job. Joe thanked him and walked back to the saloon. He ordered a beer and a whiskey.

"You got any left overs from your lunch bar?" Joe asked.

"Yup. Want some of it? Fairly dry I suspect." The bartender stated.

"Well I just got called out to head toward Bisbee and won't get any supper here. Your dried goods are better than my cooking on the trail." Joe laughed.

The bartender brought out the goods and Joe grabbed some items. The meat would be good anyway. The bartender brought a small cloth bag over and told Joe to take what he might want with him. He had to throw a lot of things out anyway. Joe ate some and gathered other stuff for the trip. He also got a bottle of 'firewater' for the trip. He thanked the man and headed back to the blacksmith's place.

CHAPTER FIVE

"How's things going Hank?" Joe asked.

"Just one last shoe to go and you can head off. I suppose you are raring to go." Hank told him.

"Sure. You been to Bisbee lately?" Joe asked.

"Not for over six years now." Hank said.

"Well that is less time than needed to forget about the place. Things are kinda rough around there anymore." Joe stated. "They must be having more Mexican bandit problems from what my telegram said."

"OK. You are ready now. Glad you had me check these. The rear shoes were getting worn on the front fairly bad. Might have lost one just on a good trail." Hank told Joe.

"Well thanks a million. See you when I get around again. Buy you a drink then." Joe said as he walked Jean outside and saddled her.

Joe mounted up and rode off to the southeast. He figured not to arrive in Bisbee until tomorrow. He smiled to himself as he wondered if Indians would invade his camp this coming night. Joe thought about what the situation might be in Bisbee. There had been trouble on and off there for years. Many of the Mexican bandits had felt Arizona was within their territory like it had been in the past. The day moved along with Joe enjoying the cool breeze. About five in the afternoon he found a campsite for the night. As normal the site had a dry river and Joe checked this out by digging down a short way. He could get water yet so he felt good here. He unsaddled Jean and let her walk around the area looking for something to eat. Joe gathered some wood and laid a fire. He would manage to eat beans and bacon again. This was better than nothing and he had seen nothing loose on his ride this day to gather for supper.

Supper was finished and Joe was relaxing by his small fire. He was enjoying the peacefulness of the area and wondered if there had ever been much activity around here. He finally laid his bedroll out and settled down for night's rest. About 1 in the morning Jean awakened Joe. She was concerned about something and she made some low whimpering noise. Joe knew enough to look around the area. The moon was bright this night and he could see fairly well. Jean was facing to the south in the camp and evidently whatever she was concerned about was out there. Slowly Joe got into a crouch to see well. He sat still and hardly breathed as he searched for the problem.

Jean now was getting more concerned and she was backing up toward Joe. He was motionless still searching the area. Jean was very nervous and he figured that humans would not be such a concern for her. Joe had his pistol in hand and then he began to see a shadow just past Jean. He stared toward the shadow and now could see it was moving very cautiously and slow toward Jean. Finally Joe saw what it was. A mountain cat had smelled Jean and was looking for a meal. This type critter generally did not get close to humans. This one might be very hungry to not worry about Joe. Joe aimed carefully at the shadow and squeezed the trigger of his six-gun. A loud report from the gun was followed by a scream from the cat. The animal jumped straight into the air about five feet and came back down. The cat was pawing the air and twisting it's body in very weird shapes. Then as fast as things had started all was quiet again. Jean seemed to know that the danger was gone. Joe slowly walked to the cat and carefully nudged it. Nothing moved so the animal probably was gone from this world. The cat was large but Joe did not think it could have killed Jean. He decided to get back into his bed and worry about things in the morning.

The dawn broke and Joe was sitting up on his bedroll. He felt good after the night's rest even with the sidetrack of the cat. He stood up and walked to the cat. It was a younger one as it appeared. It probably was hungry and had not found much to eat around this area. These animals could cost a rancher a few young calves each year. Joe was very glad he had managed to find and see the cat last night. Jean could have been badly hurt and this would ruin her for future wasteland use. Joe had some breakfast and saddled Jean up, ready for this coming day. He figured to be in Bisbee this evening.

The trail was quiet and Joe was again enjoying the ride as he moved toward his assignment. He still could not figure what might be involved once he arrived in Bisbee. Around ten this morning Joe was riding in some small hills and he knew this trail very well. A small draw was along this trail and he had been concerned in the past about being caught here by Indians. Now that was a thing of the past. He was wondering how many times Indians had watched him travel through this area. He had never had trouble however so it always seemed a safe travel area.

Suddenly some shots were fired. Joe quickly slid off Jean and let her move out of the way. He gained a spot with a few smaller rocks and looked around. He could see nothing but shots were still being fired. He finally located the area the shots were coming from as the gunfire was shown by the smoke of their rounds. It was strange since he could see the people that fired on him but they were now showing their backs to him and firing up the hill here. This was a new switch.

As Joe watched the scene many of the men were dropping and not firing. This was known by Joe to indicate their being hit by some of the firing. He wondered if this might be a cavalry patrol that had stumbled on the situation. It must be since the fire was coming from a few men as near as he could tell. Things now became quiet again. No fire was heard and no sounds either. Joe was very curious about this. He moved forward hoping to get a better sight of the situation. He slowly arrived close to the men that had fired on him. He was shocked to see these men all dead. They appeared to be Mexican men due to their dress.

He was not sure to trust the other side as to safety. He elected to sit for a few minutes watching up the hill. Soon he began seeing some movement on the hill. He finally got a good look at the other side and immediate saw they were Indians. Two of the men headed down the hill toward Joe and he hoped they were not concerned about him living yet. As the two reached Joe, one held his hand flat out and palm up to Joe. He said something but Joe did not understand. The second brave translated, telling Joe these men had been set to ambush Joe. The Indians had seen this and stepped in to eliminate the trouble. This brave told Joe he was being watched as he was considered a friend to the Indian natives.

Joe appreciated this and motioned for the two men to follow him. He walked to Jean and got some ammo from his saddlebags. He handed this to them in payment for their help. Joe knew they had trouble getting ammo at times. Indians were not considered trustworthy to handle ammo from white men. He told them he owed them more than this but it was all he had for now. The two men thanked Joe and walked back toward the hill. Joe went to the dead Mexicans and checked them out for information as to whom they were. They carried some Mexican money so they must have come up from the border. Joe did not worry about burial for these men. He figured the coyotes and buzzards needed to eat also.

Joe walked back to Jean and mounted up to move on. He thought about the situation and was glad the Indians were on his side. He could see how they had caused so much trouble in the past. They could move around a populated area and never be detected. Basically white men were not much for wasteland travel. Joe had enough excitement for the day so he didn't bother to stop for lunch. He finally topped a rise above the flat plain to the north of Bisbee. He sat and watched here for a minute. A person could see a long way over this plain. He saw a dust trail to the left of him. He could identify this as a stage moving toward Tombstone. Further to the east he could see a small group of men riding.

CHAPTER FIVE

They were riding in formation so Joe figured they were military on a patrol. It was easy to see how the Indians kept track of things in this area.

Joe moved on to the southeast now and was able to see some of the Bisbee houses on the high part of town. Bisbee was a mining town basically and many of the population here were workers in these mines. Joe figured an hour or so on to town. He would stop by the law office there and then check into a hotel for the night. He would at least learn the trouble here from the Sheriff. There were some clouds gathering in the southwestern sky but Joe knew it was not the season for any rain. These clouds generally disbursed as they came inland.

The main street of Bisbee was not showing any action as Joe rode in. There were a few horses outside a couple saloons but nothing else. Joe rode directly to the Sheriff's office and went inside.

"Hello you outlaw. I suppose you've been sitting in that chair since I left you last time." Joe said with a smile.

"What the hell are you doing back here? I thought we got rid of all the riffraff the last time." The Sheriff replied.

"Well, got a notice from headquarters that you had problems with Mexican bandits down here." Joe said. "Course I can see that you sitting in that chair all the time makes it hard to get anything done."

The two men sat and talked for a time and then Joe said he needed to get a hotel and some supper. The Sheriff agreed with the supper so they would talk during that. Joe walked to the hotel for a room and he would put Jean in the stable also. He arranged things and then walked back to the Sheriff's office. The two men walked to the café. Joe knew the menu here and the food was usually good. The two men sat down at a table and ordered a meal. The waitress brought them coffee also.

"Well, what information is burning headquarters?" Joe asked.

A WASTELAND OF OUTLAWS

"Many incidents of bandit work around this area and on through New Mexico and Texas. We have been hit with ten times normal bandit work in the last year." The Sheriff said in a lower voice.

"This is beginning to sound like a military job. Has anyone actually seen these bandits?" Joe asked.

"Nope. They see the aftermath and they leave signs, which are read by Mexican citizens around here. There have been some hints as to getting Arizona, New Mexico and other border areas back to the Mexican Government." The Sheriff said.

"I have horror thoughts of things like this. Prescott has been getting some information regarding tensions like this." Joe said.

"Just flippen great! I have heard rumors myself and I have wondered if these bandits might not be Mexican military men." The Sheriff said. "Tomorrow I will take you out to an area that has been getting hit hard by these bandits."

The two men discussed some other matters and then headed to the saloon to wash their meal down. The Sheriff here was a good man and Joe had always respected him. He had to keep peace among town people and ranchers plus adding the Mexican nationals that came around frequently. The Sheriff's budget was not made out for all this activity. He was only allowed five deputies also. A few drinks at the saloon and Joe was ready to crawl in bed and get ready for the coming day.

CHAPTER SIX

orning found Joe up and sitting in the café eating his breakfast. The Sheriff arrived shortly after Joe had entered the café and pulled up a chair at his table.

"Have a good night?" The Sheriff asked.

"Not bad. Guess it was you that kept all the noise and gun play out. Good time for a new thing for you." Joe laughed.

"If you have nothing planned after breakfast I'll take you out to see some interesting things." The Sheriff said. "You might even feel a little sorry for me after you see what I put up with around here."

The two finished their breakfast and then both walked to the stable and retrieved their horses. Jean was glad to see Joe and she was ready to go as soon as Joe would saddle her. The two mounted up and headed out west of town. There was a hilly area about 15 miles ahead and this was where the Sheriff was finding a lot of sign from bandits. Joe was watching around as they rode on. There had been a lot of activity along this trail. Must have been a large number of men working around here. Suddenly the Sheriff stopped and stared to the side of the road. Joe looked and saw a trailside alter. This was brand new according to the sheriff. People did not put such things where no one came very much. The Sheriff walked up to the alter and looked it over close. There were some candles and religious artifacts around the area. Also a sign was placed above everything. It was in Spanish and basically stated this was for grand revolution fighters. That alone would tell everyone what was happening around here. The alter probably was placed here since very few locals ever was in this area.

The two men now moved on and both were watching all around as they didn't want to get surprised by anyone. A little later they began seeing some built up areas with heavy rock structures that appeared to be for shelter from attacks. Normally a person would not create anything like this unless they expected future confrontations. This was a very interesting thing to Joe. There was nothing around this area and not any person living within ten miles as far as they knew. The military very seldom rode through this area. Some one had information about future things. This would be a thing for everyone to study and listen for. Surprises can be scary at times if they are against you. Joe made a mental note to return to Camp Huachuca after he left here. The military should be let in on some things here.

Finally the Sheriff advised they probably needed to return to Bisbee as they might get caught out here over night and he was not anxious for this. The day had been informative and both the lawmen would have to hold this information for future reference. As the two rode back to the east, Joe was watching still. He now saw things that were a relief to him. Some observers had been watching them and they were not Mexicans. The Indians made sure that Joe saw he was being watched. Joe smiled and mentioned this to the Sheriff. This was a shock to the Sheriff but he knew if Joe mentioned it things would be that way. He had never heard of any white man being protected and especially lone men out in the wastelands.

CHAPTER SIX

The two men arrived back in Bisbee about six in the evening. The sky was clouding up again here and it looked as if it could rain. Arizona did have times when generally rain did not happen. Every now and then this rule would be broken by nature. The two men rode to the café and went in for some supper. They would discuss this day later. They ordered a meal and sat back to relax after the days ride. They had just received their meal when a bunch of horses came riding down the street with a lot of yelling and gun shooting. Both the lawmen jumped up and ran outside the café. About six men were on horseback and firing their pistols in various directions. They were not firing in the air. Now the lawmen began to see that this might be a raiding party of sorts.

It didn't take long for the mounted men to notice the lawmen. A couple of shots dropped the Sheriff and Joe was already in action. He was aiming at the general group and he noticed that two of them had fallen off their horses. He continued not knowing how the Sheriff was. He managed to get two more men as he was ducking around various objects around the street. The last two men were suddenly riding hard out of town. Joe had not been hit during this fight but he knew the Sheriff had. He ran to the man and checked on him. The Sheriff was dead. Nothing left for him out of this. Joe felt bad about this since the man had been a good lawman and there had been no reason for his death.

Joe had a couple of men carry the Sheriff to the undertakers place. The man had no relatives here and as far as Joe knew he had none elsewhere either. A sad ending for a good man. Now Joe made a solemn promise to find the last two men that had been involved here. He would bring them to justice to account for the Sheriff. A couple of deputies were now taking control of the town. Joe knew them also and they both appeared to be good lawmen coming up. Joe stood along the street for a time letting the evening air assist in his pain at the loss of another human being that never should have faced such an end.

Joe began circulating among the gathering crowd. He needed to find out as much as possible about this group of men. He had already heard that these were Mexican bandits from many people. They lived across the border and came here whenever they wished. Generally they did not commit such wanton slaughter until now. Joe continued to explore what everyone had to say. Each bit of information could be very helpful for the future. The deputies managed to give Joe some information also. Evidently these men had come around in the past but never gave any sign of acting as they had this night. Joe had a suspicion that today's ride might had triggered some additional behavior.

Joe finally walked to the saloon to get some pain relief. As he arrived there were many people there and they all nodded to him. They agreed that this had been a very bad omen for the town. Joe promised to gain back the pride of the town. He managed to sit at a table and he passed the word that he would appreciate any information that anyone might have about the events this day. Joe knew that some people in town had a lot more information about things and he just hoped they would pass some of this to him. The bartender figured what Joe was looking for and he passed information on and tried to get customers he figured might know things to see Joe.

Joe spent about two hours at the saloon and he had received some information that he wanted to expand on. He now went to his hotel room for the night. He would send a wire to Prescott in the morning. He needed a week or so here now to finish this latest situation. He would have to travel across the border himself for additional facts. He could not find and arrest anyone there however and he could not legally fight and kill anyone there. He needed to get his information and return before things got too hot over there. The Mexican police were known to be somewhat rowdy themselves and

44

they always would stick up for one of their citizens against a US person. This held even more if the person was a US lawman.

The next day Joe sent his wire to headquarters and also to Camp Huachuca for Colonel Jones. He wanted enough people to know what was going on here in case he failed in neutralizing the situation. He wanted to ride to Douglas this day and talk with the law over there. He hoped someone might know information that could assist him in the investigation. The first thing today was to sit with the deputies and try to gain as much as he could from them. He would ride to Douglas after that. Joe was feeling excited about this new project he had. He knew there was much information around if only he could dig it out.

The deputies had a little more information they had remembered since last night. They still were in a fix over what would happen here in Bisbee now. The mayor had already asked one of them to take the job of Sheriff and this had been agreed on by both these men. The information at this time indicated that these outlaws had been working both sides of the border for a time. They seemed to have become concerned yesterday when the Sheriff and Joe had been seen returning to Bisbee from the west. There must have been something that neither Joe nor the Sheriff had seen that direction. So this was a new lead. There had been enough concern that he and the Sheriff had been attacked last night. Joe now figured he needed to be much more alert around here.

Joe next rode to Douglas and hoped to find additional information there. He arrived and went to the Marshal's office. He sat down and talked with this man for a time and for some reason he felt there was an underlining current here. The Marshal was not giving out much information and Joe was sure he knew more than he was telling. After a few minutes, Joe thanked the Marshal and walked down the street. He entered the saloon on the street and sat at a table toward the rear. There was some concern here now as customers seemed to be unhappy to be close to Joe. Joe was trying to figure things out while he sat here. He was not concerned about the way people were acting but he was concerned about the whole town.

Joe had been sitting at the table about 30 minutes and the back door opened just a crack. Joe did not miss this and was fully engaged in watching this if a gun would slowly come through the crack. The door opened more and Joe saw a hand just outside and it beckoned him to come. He looked around the place and evidently no one else had noticed this signal. He quietly got up and walked out the front of the saloon. He did not want to get anyone in trouble if this was an information witness. If not, he wanted to be on his own grounds when meeting someone that might want to shoot him.

Joe eased around the corner of the saloon building and walked softly to the back. Here he looked around the corner and saw a man standing there close to the back door. Joe stepped out into full view of the man and spoke.

"You want to see me?" Joe said.

The man jumped at the sound of the words. He looked scared at Joe and then nodded. Joe walked closer to him.

"What's on your mind?" Joe asked.

The man looked around and then seemed to feel everything was ok yet.

"I have some information for you that may enlighten you about what has happened." The man said.

Joe looked at the man for a moment and he could see the man was not comfortable yet. Joe walked closer to him and he looked the man straight in the eyes. The man blinked and looked over his shoulder again.

"Last night was a planned incident. Those six men are Mexican Nationals and they work both sides of the place. The Sheriff had been getting too far into possible problems ahead and this was the key to getting him out of the picture.

CHAPTER SIX

When you two rode back into town yesterday from the west, they figured things had to end. You were to be killed also but things did not work out well for them." The man told Joe. "All these bandits from Mexico are really revolutionary soldiers planning to not only take their country over but to get back New Mexico and Arizona."

Now Joe was seeing a new light on things. "Anyone on this side going along with all this?" Joe asked.

The man looked around again and then stated, "Most of the law in Douglas is somewhat involved. There are a lot of people in town going along with everything. Bisbee has been a thorn to them for over a year. The Sheriff was strongly against all this but he really didn't know what was going on."

"Well we had better not be seen together here. Come to my hotel room after seven tonight. We can talk better there." Joe told the man.

The man nodded and turned around to leave. He made it to the edge of the saloon building and a shot from the front street was heard. A bullet found it's mark and the man dropped dead. Something very bad was coming around here as best as Joe could see. He checked the man and then waited for the deputies. They came on a run and immediately saw what happened. They asked Joe to come to the office with them as they didn't want to be next on the list by the killer.

Joe turned around and walked the other direction to help the deputies keep themselves clear of any suspicion. Each one walked a different way to the office. One had to get the coroner for the body of the dead man and he also had to appear as if investigating the crime. He entered the saloon and asked questions about this. The only thing he got was that the Ranger had been in the saloon just prior to the incident and had walked out the front. This had probably dropped all thoughts that the Ranger had anything to do with this man. Someone had known this man knew something and was afraid he might tell the Ranger.

Now Joe was a bit gun shy about telling anyone what he knew. The man had indicated that the law in Douglas might know things so Joe was not sure who might be on his side. He really didn't trust the deputies at this time. They sat in the office and discussed things.

"Did you talk with this man before he was shot?" One deputy asked Joe.

"No, didn't have a chance. I was in the saloon and left to check on my horse. I came around the saloon building and was going to walk to the stable. That poor man was already there and he got himself shot." Joe told them.

"Well too bad. He might have had some information about last night. Can't figure any other reason for him being shot." The other deputy said.

"Well if you hear anything I would be obliged if you might let me know. I still need information and it seems there isn't much around here." Joe said. "I'll be around for the day then I have to move to Camp Huachuca."

Joe walked out of the office and had very mixed emotions now about everything that was going on here. He went to his hotel room. He needed to lay back and think of what was happening here. Joe had never been involved in such a mess. He did think that Camp Huachuca might send a group here to watch over things for a few weeks.

CHAPTER SEVEN

Joe met the next day with uncertainty. He had not obtained any more information after last night. He was at a loss to understand anything of what was going on around here. He decided to ride around the mine here and find whatever he could from it. The mine was a huge affair and it was so profitable that the owners were shipping ore back east for milling. Joe knew from the past that Mexico City had a smelter for cooper. It might be a profitable venture to them obtaining the mines in this area for sales worldwide. Cooper was a very valuable product at this time. This put another point up for the cause of an attempt to gain back this area.

Joe talked with the deputies again this morning and he was still very guarded to what he said. He felt a huge barrier between him and them now. He would ride off later this day and see what might be around away from here. He needed to sit with the Colonel and discuss things. The Colonel was strong on information and he many informants for keeping tabs on local things.

A WASTELAND OF OUTLAWS

Joe finally saddled Jean and bid the deputies bye for now. He was up and riding early and he figured he could get a good way toward Camp Huachuca before night. He would push fairly hard since he did not feel safe around this area now. People might get the idea that he was finding things and he could be a target like the Sheriff and the other man. The day was good at any rate and Jean was enjoying getting out on the trail. She always seemed to like moving along. Joe had left the door open when he left Bisbee however. He was sure he would return here before long. Too many things were still in the air and he needed to get some solid information.

Joe rode along and he kept watch on the high points. He had always managed this against danger to his own life. Now he felt good, as he would see glimpses of Indians at times. He knew they were watching him. He was very glad this was added into his ventures. Joe wanted to look over the area he and the Sheriff had been around before. He would try to get a patrol from the camp to go with him. He would not be in shape to ride this area alone. There was way too much around there to be concerned about for now.

The day past uneventful and Joe reached an area to camp for the night. He set down and took care of Jean then set up his bedroll and fire ring. He would only have beans this night, as he had not obtained much for trail chow. He started his small fire and heated the beans, which was better than cold ones all the time. He sat after eating and listened to the night sounds as nocturnal animals came awake and began their daily activities. Finally Joe lay down and looked at the stars. He always felt a sense of security under the stars. They seemed to be his personal ceiling.

The night passed and Joe was up heating his beans and making coffee again. He had a good sleep this last night and was anxious to get on to Camp Huachuca. He finished his coffee and then cleaned up the area a little. He saddled Jean and they were off. The day was bright with no clouds around. As Joe started moving out, he saw something that

CHAPTER SEVEN

was different in the area of the camp. He stopped and looked things over. Finally he dismounted again and walked around the area a little. He had a sudden wave of anxiety as he came upon a body that was drug under a mesquite bush. The man had been killed with a knife and a partial scalp had been removed. This brought Joe immediately into the awareness of the area all around. He cautiously edged around the area and he found more bodies. He counted seven in all and they had been killed in the same way. Each body was only about a hundred yards or so from his camp. He now realized that the Indians had protected him again. He finally found an arrow stuck in a tree, which was a sign of credit for the Indians braves.

Evidently some men had traveled out to take him during the night. He had no knowledge of all this and the braves must have seen the other men headed toward his camp. Joe stood and thought for a few minutes and then he figured the braves might be watching him yet. He dug into his saddlebags and pulled out some boxes of ammo again. He had restocked this in Bisbee and now was glad he had. Joe stood in an open area and held his arms up with boxes in each hand. This would be a sign to the braves of a thank you and a gift of the ammo. Joe laid the boxes on a large rock there and mounted Jean to ride on.

The rest of the trip went without problems and Joe would have some good stories to tell the Colonel and Hank both at Huachuca. He didn't really know why but the Indians were strongly protecting him. He did not figure the arrest of the rustlers was worth all this however. He was very pleased at any rate and he would think of what might be a good repayment for all this security. The gifts of ammo was a sign to the Indians that Joe knew they had saved him and this would be a bit of pride for them.

Joe rode into the camp just after noon. He tied Jean up outside the headquarters building and walked inside. Here the sergeant met him.

"The Colonel is gone for now Joe. He wasn't expecting you at any rate." The sergeant told him.

"OK, I'll be over at the saloon if he has time to see me." Joe told the sergeant.

"He should be back in three or four hours." The sergeant said. "I'll tell him when he gets back."

Joe walked back outside and took Jean to the blacksmith.

"Hello Joe. Got time for me to check those new shoes?" Hank asked.

"Sure do. I believe I should be around the rest of the day." Joe told him. "I'm going to the saloon. Buy you a drink later if you stop by."

Joe walked to the saloon and stood at the bar.

"Well Joe you didn't stay gone very long. Get lonesome for the good ol army?" The bartender asked.

"Oh sure. Can't stand to be away from this place and miss out on your rotten whiskey." Joe laughed.

Joe stood at the bar talking with the bartender. There were no other people here right now. This was a consistent thing, as the soldiers were not allowed here during the day. Joe had been here about 45 minutes and a sergeant came in. He walked to Joe and nodded to the bartender.

"I got some interesting information about you Joe." The sergeant said. "Seems one of our scouts was visiting some of his family with a local tribe bunch and you came up on conversation."

"Really? What did they want my bad hair?" Joe laughed.

"Nope, seems you are a hero to these people. Don't know what you did but they hold you in a high light." The sergeant said.

"I've noticed that they are always watching me on the trail. They even managed to take out seven men last night that were up to no good around my camp. Didn't know it till morning." Joe mentioned.

CHAPTER SEVEN

"According to our scout, Happy Eagle, most of the braves around would give their lives up to save you." The sergeant said. "Never heard of such."

"Wow, that is something. Can't understand why this all would come about." Joe said.

"It seems the tribe has been watching you for four or five years. They think you are a grand spirit person that is sent to help them." The sergeant said. "You must have really did something great for them."

"Unknowingly I might have but nothing I remember." Joe said.

"Well, I have to get back to work. Just wanted to let you know." The sergeant said. He walked out the door.

"That is sure something." The bartender said. "I wouldn't have believed it but the sergeant never spreads rumors."

Joe had a couple more drinks here and then left to see about Jean. He was still bothered about what he might have done for the Indians. He knew of nothing that would rate this high of a repayment. Hank had checked Jean out and she was fine now. He told Joe to put her in a stall and give her some good oats. Joe appreciated all this and he liked to treat Jean. She was a very good horse and had never let him down. A runner came to the blacksmiths and told Joe the Colonel was back and wanted to see him. Joe thanked him and walked to the headquarters.

The colonel was in the main part of the front room when Joe walked in.

"Hello Joe. Glad you made it back in one piece. Come into the office." The Colonel said.

They walked inside the office and the Colonel closed the door. He got a couple of glasses out and poured them a liberal drink. They sat and talked and Joe recanted the last couple of days to him. He had been thinking of something going on down there also. He was glad that Joe had been assigned to cover this. He was not sure how far his authority might extend toward this thing. At least for now he could step in until there were actual indications of trouble. Joe asked if a patrol could be formed to go with him to the south and check the area again where he and the Sheriff had been the day he was killed. The colonel was not sure but he would consider this and get back to Joe. The two talked for almost an hour and then Joe left to send a wire back to Prescott.

Joe left the Colonel and now got Jean to ride off the post. There was a small saloon outside the post and he might get some information by listening to people there. He walked inside the saloon and there were about six people there. Joe took a table to relax and listen. The six men must have been working together and had some time off now. Joe began picking up some of their conversation. They had been watching things and it seemed that Mexican Nationals were coming across the border at regular intervals. They would ride around areas and look at things. They did not go into the Huachuca Mountains to the west of the post however. They seemed to be concerned about Indians living there. There was a lake on the west side of these mountains that was considered as holy by the Indians. They were very active in guarding this area and no one wanted to be caught around there.

This information was very interesting to Joe. He remembered a few years ago that he was working in these mountains and had come across some white men camping there. He checked them out and found they were outlaws wanted by Tucson. He had arrested them and removed them from the area. They had been chopping trees down and making living areas there. Maybe this was one of the things the Indians had seen about Joe. One of the men here had talked with some Mexican Nationals last week and they were pushing him to tell them if he would support an uprising to take this area back into Mexican hands. Things were going well here at the saloon and Joe sat listening for an hour. He had picked up many things from the men talking and now he

CHAPTER SEVEN

would return and discuss things with the Colonel. He also figured to go back to Tombstone and see what he might hear there.

Joe returned to the camp and went directly to the telegraph office. He had a message from headquarters and they were hearing many things similar to what he had. This was the concern they had and sent him to see about such. He sent a wire back to them and covered most things at present. Joe next walked back to headquarters. He found the Colonel still in and willing to see him again. They sat in the office and talked for an hour and a half this time. The Colonel was seeing things now that were coming together from Joe's information. The Colonel agreed that Joe should go to Tombstone next and see what was cropping up around there.

Joe stopped by the small store at the camp and gathered some chow for his trip. He only expected to need two meals plus some snacks. He usually tried to carry enough in case he got caught somewhere and couldn't get to a town as soon as he expected. He planned on camping this first night along the San Pedro River again. This would still allow him to reach Tombstone the next day. There was some mighty barren land between the San Pedro and Tombstone so Joe didn't want to get caught anywhere around there at night.

A WASTELAND OF OUTLAWS

CHAPTER EIGHT

oe rode out of Camp Huachuca and headed to the east. He knew this route fairly well as he traveled it more than most trails in his district. He was very anxious to get to Tombstone and see what he might hear there. As he rode along he thought of all that had happened over the last few days. He could definitely see why this situation might become a monster and cause problems over a large area. If the Mexican authorities were involved in this plan then the US would have to step in and get things stopped. If war started with Mexico Joe figured the US should be able to stomp it out immediately. They might have to get additional troops however. Fort Bowie and Camp Huachuca were the closest military places at this time. Joe hoped that a war could be prevented and it probably would depend on the people right around here. Most of the people here were against repossession by Mexico.

Joe arrived at the San Pedro and set down for the night. He built his fire ring and unsaddled Jean. She knew this area now also. There was generally good green grass around from growing near the water. Joe sat and watched the area for a while and studied a squirrel that was going about its business. There were not many nuts or seeds for the little critters but somehow they managed to survive and raise small families. Joe felt a peace of mind here. He also was relaxed knowing what the Indians had done to him here. The word was out and Joe had been surprised about the information from the scout at Camp Huachuca. Things were quiet and peaceful here.

The next morning found Joe back on the trail headed to Tombstone. He would be there by mid afternoon. He kept watch as he rode along and saw nothing. In this area a person could generally see for miles unless a small hill blocked the view. Joe always watched the various mining claims that could be seen in this area. A lot of mines had been staked and then run dry. Many men had lost about all they had working these worthless places. A few had made good money however and this seemed to push new men into prospecting for riches. Tombstone finally came into view about 3. Joe rode directly in and headed for the Marshal's office.

Joe was welcomed back and the Marshal asked him how things were going. Joe eased into the situation but did not give all his information out. He wanted to see just how this man was set in thinking. He had known the Marshal for about three years and considered him an honest man. He had taken over from the Earps and was running the town in perfect condition. There were very few shooting now days. The two bounced things around for a few minutes and then the Marshal suggested they go to the saloon and see what they might hear. Joe was in favor of this. So far the Marshal had no indication of anything running around here in regards to Joe's problem.

The two lawmen sat down at a table and the bartender brought over a bottle and glasses. He welcomed Joe back and told them to enjoy. Joe sat at the table and felt relaxed. He didn't care right now if nothing worked out. He had always liked Tombstone and usually felt at home here. The two sat and did talk in lower voices about some things but mostly they were listening. If they heard anything interesting the Marshal could get the person to come over and give them the info. The two sat in the saloon about an hour and nothing was heard. The Marshal figured nighttime would be better for getting any good information. They walked out and made a patrol of the town. This gave Joe some exercise.

"Well, I need to get some boring paperwork finished Joe. I'll meet you at the saloon later." The Marshal said.

"OK, see you then. Joe walked to the saloon and got a table again. He would get some Mexican food here as they had about the best. Joe was feeling fine here and when his food came it was good. He watched people as he ate and finally most people were gone. They probably had to get home if they were married. Joe finished his meal and was drinking a beer now. A man came in the door and looked around. He saw Joe sitting at the table and walked directly to him. He did not sit down but leaned over a little and looked at Joe.

"I have some good information about some things around here. I thought you should know. The man spoke softly. "There is a thing happening all over this area and it is involved with Mexican -------------"

A shot rang out from the door of the saloon. The man standing at Joe's table fell across it dead. He had been killed and probably because of what he was going to tell Joe. Joe jumped up and ran outside. He could see nothing in the street or on the boardwalk. Some people began sticking their heads out now to see what was happening. Whatever the information it was sealed within the dead man. The Marshal arrived at the saloon and asked Joe what happened? Joe told him. The Marshal shook his head. This man was a recorder at the courthouse here. He had a lot of inside information as to what was going on around the area. This was especially true about land dealings. Joe was very confused now and it seemed that maybe he was not very healthy to be around anymore. People were getting killed around him and did not even know why.

Joe took a couple of hard slugs of whiskey and sat down. He was looking at the saloon door. Usually Tombstone people were around when there was shooting and someone always saw who was shot and whom the gunman was. This incident had not yielded anyone with information. Joe was definitely confused now. As the last few days had went by this problem seemed to be growing and not mellowing down. Joe was sure now that he would be a regular target for the one side of the issue. The other side might have more people that really did not want to get involved. People were like this and such inactivity created problems that allowed the bad guys to promote their mission.

"I'm going to take a short survey around Joe. I'll be back here shortly." The Marshal said.

"Ok. I think I just want to sit here for a few minutes. Things are happening so fast I don't even know where everything is coming from." Joe stated.

Joe poured another drink and sat looked out the door with more a stare than anything else. He was almost in a state of shock over things. The saloon had cleared out and no one was interested in seeing Joe anymore. The bartender even appeared to be jumpy. Whatever was happening it was large enough to cover most of Joe's area. Right now Joe just sat and waited for the Marshal to return. He wouldn't blame the man for staying away now. Joe felt like getting drunk but he also knew that in this stage he would be easy prey. So far no one had tried to take him out so he didn't want to encourage anyone further.

Now Joe wanted to send a wire off to headquarters so he walked outside and toward the telegraph office. He needed to keep headquarters informed as to what was happening down here. If he did get taken out they at least

CHAPTER EIGHT

would have a little information to start someone else going here. Whatever was raising its cruel head had the grasp on the area and was very big. Joe sent a wire to headquarters and to Camp Huachuca also. The Colonel might be a last chance for Joe at any time. He wanted the man to know what he did as things came. Joe kept a good watch around him as he walked. This was getting worse than riding out in the wasteland. Joe knew he would be much safer out there with the Indians watching over him.

Joe walked back to the saloon hoping to see the Marshal again soon. He might have some good information. The Marshal entered the saloon a few minutes after Joe returned.

"Well, I don't know what is going on but the town is sure in a lockdown it seems. I couldn't get to first base with anyone." The Marshal told Joe. "You got any information about all this?"

"Not a drop. Just seems that I am a very unhealthy person to be around. Maybe you should take that to heart." Joe said.

"I had a different incident just a few minutes ago. I was talking with the General Store owner and for a minute it seemed he was on the verge of telling me something. Then a man walked in the place and the owner shutdown and I couldn't get him back." The Marshal said.

"Do you know anyone outside of town that might have some good information?" Joe asked. "I could ride out and check things out maybe."

"Kinda scary though isn't it?" The Marshal said. "I don't think you are much for collecting information. Not bad for corpses however."

"Yeah, guess your right." Joe sighed.

"Maybe I could do some work for you outside town. I go out many times a week so it wouldn't look bad." The Marshal said.

"You sure you want to try that?" Joe asked. "I could be dangerous for you as well."

"Never know until I try. I've been shot at before so that wouldn't be my first party!" The Marshal stated.

The two sat for a few more minutes then decided to get some chow. They walked to the café. The owner there saw them come in and he got a shocked look on his face. He didn't seem very anxious to see the two in his place. The Marshal did not miss this. A man had to eat and this should not be seen by anyone as an information-gathering episode. The Marshal figured he would ride off in the morning and see what he might find. Meanwhile Joe thought it might be a good idea for the Marshal to stay away from him. So they finished eating and then split up. They agreed the Marshal should patrol the town and Joe should sit in the saloon. Joe had thoughts that he might be safer to camp out but he enjoyed his comfortable bed too much.

Joe sat drinking in the saloon until about eight. He then decided to go to the hotel. He went to his room and carefully secured things there. He arranged things to help him stay healthy if he was attacked. The window overlooked the main street but it had no balcony. The only way a person could get in the room was through the door. Joe carefully moved the bed over closer to the door. He put a rod from the closet between the bed and the door. This would allow him to get notification if anyone was trying to come in. He would get a jolt and he would be able to roll off the bed to meet whatever was coming in the room. It would take two or three strong hits on the door to move the bed enough to allow entrance.

Joe climbed into his bed and stared at the ceiling for a time. He was still wondering what everything was tying into. There was a main pivot point for all this but where? He had his pistol by his pillow and was hoping it wouldn't be needed. He finally dozed off. About 3 Joe was brought awake with some gunfire on the main street below. He jumped out of bed and looked cautiously down. Two men were involved in a shoot out there and nothing more. Joe watched the two for a short time and then climbed back in bed. He slept well and awoke as the sun was climbing into daylight.

Today Joe wanted to go to the courthouse and look around. He figured the man that was killed yesterday trying to tell him something had found problems in the file system at the courthouse. After breakfast Joe told the Marshal where he was going. The Marshal seemed to think as Joe but he wasn't anxious to be there with Joe. Joe understood this and he went by himself. He was met with cold greetings at the courthouse. He asked to look at some of the records on file and the woman was not ready to let him look.

"You will need permission to look in these files." The woman told him.

"Who to I see to get this permission?" Joe asked.

The woman told him to check with the commissioner down the hall. Joe thanked her and walked there. He talked with the man for a few minutes and got permission for Joe to look in the files. The commissioner told Joe that he had rights to anything here since he was an Arizona Ranger. Joe walked back to the files.

"Ok, I have permission and you should have known that before." Maybe you are trying to hide something or just are damn mean in your personality." Joe snapped at her.

The women bowed her head slightly and walked out of the office. Joe went to work with the files. He had no idea what he was looking for but he looked with a systematic search. He was going through files as he sat on a low chair by the file boxes. He heard a very slight shuffle behind him and he reacted instantly. He drew his gun and whirled around. A man was standing there ready to give him a headache with a large club. Joe almost shot in reaction but now gained his control again.

"Put the club down jerk." Joe told him.

"You are nosing where you shouldn't. I have to calm you down some." The man said as he stepped forward with his right foot. He started the swing with the club and he was checking into St. Peter's gate next.

The commissioner came running, as did a couple other office personnel.

"What happened?" The commissioner asked.

"That guy was getting ready to bean me with that club. He won't have to worry about that anymore." Joe said.

"Hell, that's George from downstairs." The commissioner said. "Why was he up here?"

"He must have been told by someone." Joe said. He looked behind the commissioner and saw the clerk that had been in the office when he first arrived.

"That woman there left here when I came back from your office commissioner." Joe said.

"I've been watching her and many odd things have been jumping up around her. Guess she in working with others more than with us. The commissioner said. "Nancy, you're fired. Get you crap out of here.

Nancy looked as if the club had hit her. She couldn't believe she had been fired. She looked at Joe. "You jerk! Hope you die a very hard way!" She stomped out of the room.

CHAPTER NINE

Joe stood there now with a question on his face. He next decided to clear the room and continue with his search. There must be something in here that would tell stories. Everyone one left the room except one woman that the commissioner asked to assist Joe, as he needed.

"Thanks. I will let you know when I am done." Joe told the man.

Joe started in again where he had been when the man tried to club him. The woman was watching him and she made a strong noise as if trying to clear her throat. Joe looked at her. He saw she was not really looking at him but she kicked her foot against a file cabinet. He wasn't sure but got the idea she was showing him something. He walked to the file cabinet and started in there. This cabinet was registrations of land around the area. Many of these records were fairly new. They had ownership of various pieces of land to some very prominent people around this area. As Joe dug into the files he found special Spanish Land Grants from years back. The dates indicated they had been issued back when the Spanish were still controlling this area. The problem that Joe could see these papers were very new. Many had been wrinkled up and then pressed back out to allow the deeds to appear old. This didn't work with anyone that knew the difference in paper from far back and now.

Joe looked at the woman in the office and smiled at her. She winked and looked away. She did not want it known she might have helped Joe. Joe got a pencil and some paper and began writing names and locations down from these files. He would need this. He was not sure but it appeared to him that the entire town of Bisbee was under one Land Grant. This would mean that some person owned the town and the mines. This was very worthwhile. Joe spent about an hour more at the files then thanked the woman and walked to the commissioner's office. He thanked the man and walked outside again. He automatically looked around and he now saw a few people scattered around staring at him. They must be scouts to watch him.

Joe walked to the telegraph office and sent a wire to headquarters. This telegram was sent in a secret code that Rangers used when they didn't want information to get out. Next he walked to the Marshal's office. He sat down and the two men talked for a time. Finally Joe decided it was time to see how the Marshal was standing. Joe told him some of the information about the files but not a lot. He was checking to see if things were standing with him and partly on the other side. Joe let some information out and then looked at the Marshal.

"What do you think about this?" Joe asked.

"Looks like we have some good information and will need to get to work about it." The Marshal said.

"What can we do?" Joe asked.

"I have been wondering about old Spanish Land Grants getting involved with this new push to get our areas back under Mexican rule." The Marshal said.

CHAPTER NINE

Now Joe was seeing what he wanted. He had not mentioned the Land Grants to the Marshal and this was his free addition to the files at the courthouse. A man couldn't get on the other side of the fence if he gave these thoughts out.

"How do we start to wind this stuff up?" Joe asked.

"I think notification of the army at Camp Huachuca would be a good starting point. We will need some strong people on our side. This is surely why everyone was getting killed by talking to you." The Marshal said.

"Good, I'll go right now and wire the camp and ask for some soldiers to get here for general protection of not only us but the good people here also." Joe said.

Joe walked to the telegraph office and sent the plain wire off. He had learned just enough code to tell if the correct message was being sent. The clerk here tapped out the message and told Joe it was sent.

"Good. Now you send it right. Don't try that gibberish again or I might just shoot you for fun." Joe told the clerk.

Joe had no idea what the clerk had sent, but the address was not right for Camp Huachuca. The clerk swallowed hard and began sending again. This time the address sounded correct. The clerk would never know that Joe really couldn't read much code however. Joe told the clerk to get a hold of him when an answer came back. Joe walked back to the Marshal's office. He was having a heavy day it seemed. About all they could do now was wait and see what might come around next. Joe was thinking a Federal Marshal would be handy to have around here now. Joe had most authority regarding the law but some Federal laws were out of his reach. He could always charge by Territory Law and then have a Federal man recharge with the other side.

In reality, Joe had no idea what the next step should be. He would have a hard time proving the land grants were new. He had seen that the other side had many people behind it. For now the best thing would be to wait for the cavalry.

Joe hoped that the colonel would come over also. The Marshal and Joe sat in the office and discussed things. They almost wore out some actions as they went over them many times. Finally they agreed to get some peace in a local saloon. Actually they were sure that things would be hidden now since the clerk at the telegraph office would surely pass information on. This might be a quiet time now until the cavalry arrived. The two lawmen began to drown their problems with some good whiskey.

The saloon had a few customers and none seemed to notice or be concerned about the lawmen now. The word had been given evidently and the password was "stay cool". Joe swore a promise to himself to continue very alert and sleep with the security of the room. He also would try not to be lulled into a false sense of security with the average people around here. He felt he had tested the Marshal and he had passed. There was only so much a person could do to allow the trust of a person.

A message came from Camp Huachuca about 4. The runner found Joe at the saloon and delivered it. The message was directly from Colonel Jones. He was coming himself and two troops of his best. He mentioned that this was some hot and heavy stuff now. The cavalry should be here by mid day tomorrow. Joe was very pleased now. He sat at the table and let his mind wonder on. This incident was rapidly turning into a traitor-laden situation. At the least people involved would be charged with sedition. Things would have to be gained to prove most of this but Joe figured that once the word was out then people would be much easier to convince them to testify against the leaders at the least.

Joe knew he would have to travel to Bisbee also to wrap everything up. The cavalry should go there also. In fact Joe was thinking that maybe a troop could head that way once they arrived here. He felt the action around Tombstone would not be very heavy. Bisbee probably was on the top of the list of traitors. Now Joe was just going to set around and wait for the cavalry. The Marshal seemed pleased also. The two men spun a lot of yarns over the next few hours. They were finally relaxed and things were looking fairly good.

As normal here some gunfire was heard down the street. The Marshal and Joe jumped up to see what was going on. A group of about ten riders came hooten into town and they were firing in the air as they rode. The Marshal stood out in the street now and he planned to stop these cowboys. They probably had just been paid and were let off to blow some steam. The ten men rode up to the Marshal and the leader stopped and looked at the lawman.

"You just standing there wondering if we might shot you?" The man asked.

"Well I really just wanted you to remember that gun play and wearing firearms in town is illegal." The Marshal said.

"Well, if we shoot you then things will be legal, right?" The leader spoke.

"Might be a little difficult to enjoy the new legal things after your dead. That is what you are about seconds away from." Joe spoke.

The leader whirled around. He had not seen Joe by the door. He figured things were out now since this ranger had his gun drawn.

"Okay, guess you can wait till later Marshal." The man said.

"Not good enough. I am tired of you jerks running everything as you want. Now ride right on out of town and don't come back." Joe spoke.

"You can bet your sweet rear I ain't riding out." The leader said.

"Fine with me. Die in your saddle then. I really don't care." Joe spoke as he raised his pistol and cocked it.

The leader got a very strange look on his face now. He was caught and had lost there was no question. He looked back at the others and he was not getting support from them either.

"Well, you moving or getting dead here?" Joe asked. "I've had my belly full of ass's like you. You can ride out and never come back or set down roots in boot hill"

The man suddenly slumped in his saddle and slowly headed his horse down the street. The other men with him asked if they had to leave also.

"You all think the same as that man?" Joe asked.

"No Sir. We just want to have a few drinks and stay out of trouble." One man answered.

"I'm sure the Marshal won't mind if you do that. No more trouble or I might put you in the same hole with your friend." Joe told them.

The riders walked their mounts to the saloon and tied them up outside. They also unhooked their pistol belts and put them over the saddle horns.

"Well we must be finished for now. Guess I should make a round and see if the rest of town is quiet and peaceful." The Marshal said.

"Well, guess I might check in the room and get some rest if possible. Tomorrow will be a full day with the army here." Joe said. He walked to the hotel.

CHAPTER TEN

Surprising the night passed peaceful. Joe had a good rest and was ready for the day now. He walked to the café and found the Marshal already having his breakfast.

"You must be getting too much rest. You are beginning to act like a banker. Come to work late and go home early." The Marshal said to Joe.

"Sure I know. You get a little bit of help and then you are ready to cash all your chips in." Joe replied. He sat down at the table.

Joe ordered ham and eggs and sat looking at the street. There was only the normal activity now.

"Think we will have any trouble today?" Joe asked.

"Hard to tell but things seem to be running on a lower key." The Marshal answered. "I really think the telegraph operator spread some of the news about."

The two men ate and then headed back the Marshal's office. They needed to get some names set regarding leadership in this insurrection. Things would move along as soon as they had grabbed a few of the men in charge. Joe was curious about Bisbee also. If the news ran fast they might lose some of the men involved there. They could run across the border and wait until things settled down.

The planning continued by the two lawmen and they finally were fairly well set for the cavalry to arrive. A lot of the names for the leadership were set by the information in the courthouse paper work. Joe also wanted to set a charge of murder against these men regarding the killing of the court clerk. A lot of charges would be dropped later as the investigation cleared some men. Others would be held for trial, probably in Tucson. The Marshal was concerned as to how they would secure the arrested men since his jail was not large. He had three cells and could handle only about eight men if they were stuffed in the place.

Just after lunch the cavalry rode into town. The Colonel wanted to enter like this to get the show of force and hopefully to take any extra wind out of the leaders sails. A feeling of excitement flowed down the main street and many people were watching out windows and doors. The Colonel rode to the Marshal's office and stopped there. The bugler held his horse and the rest of the troops remained mounted. Joe and the Marshal welcomed Colonel Jones and they sat for a few minutes talking about regular things. Then the Colonel needed to find out the best place for his men to camp. The Marshal told him the best place that had water and such for a temporary camp. The Colonel stepped back out and called a Lieutenant in to tell him where to go. He released the troops to the Lieutenant and the men moved out toward the camp. Now the Colonel asked about a good saloon to pry the dust out with. Joe jumped at this and they all headed out.

At the saloon the three men joked around and acted as if there was nothing important going around here. The bartender smiled, as he knew what the three were actually doing. A feeling of no concern could be seen by several people involved in the problem. The three men were putting on a good show. Slowly Joe began setting the situation up to

CHAPTER TEN

the Colonel. He talked in a way to not spill the beans if anyone came too close to them. The Colonel wanted to wait until tomorrow to begin with arrests and this would give the Marshal time to set up a temporary holding area. The troops would be able to guard the arrested men and the Marshal would get permission to use the basement of a local church for their jail.

Now Joe asked the Colonel about getting some men to Bisbee for a similar roundup. The Colonel advised he could send one of his troops there and Joe would only have to ride there himself to make arrests. The lawmen in Bisbee were still in question so Joe would be basically on his own until everyone's true colors were shown. Joe wanted to get things squared here in Tombstone before Bisbee. The telegraph would have to be shut down for most use here. Some of the cavalry could ride in patrols to intercept anyone trying to get to Bisbee for warning people there. Things would get going early in the morning, as Joe needed to get all this cleaned up as best he could.

This evening all the headmen here needed to meet and get a plan for the morning. The Marshal's office was the place chosen. Joe and the Marshal were telling the Colonel about some of the recent happenings here. Some of the things almost seemed impossible. The key to the entire investigation had been the finding of information at the courthouse. Everything started falling into place then. The men sat in the saloon and had another drink. Then they figured to split up until supper. Joe wanted to get cleaned up and the Colonel had to get things planned with his men about tomorrow.

Joe went to the hotel and managed to get into a bathtub. He wasn't there but a few minutes when he heard a lot of racket out in the street. A fire had started in a house only a block from the Main Street. This could be very disastrous in a town like this. Many towns had burnt to the ground after a small fire started to burn a house. Joe jumped out of the tub and dried off. He pulled his clothes on rapidly then hurried outside. The town had met the call for help and people were running all over the place. Tombstone had no regular fire department so bucket brigades were all that was available. The fire had eaten a good share of the house by this time and it seemed ready to jump to the next food supply.

The population of the town was basically in the streets now and everyone was working a hard sweat up. Water was not sufficient to stem the hard burning fire. It wasn't long before a house next door was burning also. The flames licked the house siding and as this was only cheap wood it didn't take long for this house to be eaten. Things were looking very bad now. The men worked at full capacity to halt the path of the fire and they were loosing the battle. A couple of men now manned a pump on the side street to fill a trough to get water closer to the fire. More buckets were coming now and the General Store opened up for anyone to grab buckets there. Anything that could be used was offered by the store. Joe was in the midst of hauling water also. At times like this the town forgot all other problems and mended together to fight the monster.

Within 45 minutes the fire had licked up four houses and the people could only hope things would slow it down. The men began to loose the ambition to fight as hard as they had started. A person could not give full energy out for long period like this. It was beginning to look as if the town could be lost. The fifth and sixth houses were under attack now from the fire. As the bucket brigade switched to the sixth house, the fire seemed to die down. It just lost its momentum and slowly disappeared into the black wood. There was no reason the fire shut down but everyone was very thankful for this. Slowly the people started to clean up things. Six families had been put out of a home and they would have to find somewhere to set up living rooms again. People around the town were already offering rooms and other things that the victims needed.

CHAPTER TEN

The soldiers had been sent into town to assist with the fire also. They had been a very big help. Now as things died down, the Colonel gave word for the men to be allowed some time at the saloons. He also figured on this. Joe and the Marshal soon found him and they headed to a saloon. This had been a wild late afternoon. Joe had wasted his time in the bath as everyone else had. The town would be under a blanket of despair from the tragedy and it would require many weeks to pull themselves back from the black hole this had left them. Joe sat and drank a beer while he watched everyone come and go from the saloon. It seemed everyone who had been involved was worn thin.

The night wore on slowly and the men finally were able to get some supper. It was closing in on time to get ready for the coming day. Joe talked with the two other men and he was concerned about bringing all this coming trouble at this time. The Colonel did mention that the trouble had been brought on by the people involved so it would not be on the shoulders of the good guys. In fact he wondered if this might be a needed turning point for the town. They could be brought down to see that they had some bad times other than the fire.

"I figure we should get moving at least by nine in the morning." Joe stated.

"Yes at least by then. Maybe we can weed out some individuals living out a way. Once we start, things will really get moving." The Colonel stated.

"There isn't much chance of country people getting word before we get to them. With the cavalry moving around the town things will be held quietly." The Marshal said.

"I think we can wait for the country crooks until we get the town wrapped up." Joe stated.

"Well I think it is getting toward the time to turn in and catch some sleep before the sun comes around again." The Marshal said.

"I'm going to sit here and have another drink. I've been watching some of these people and they seem to be a little jumpy with us around." Joe said. "Wonder if some might have guessed what is coming."

"Well, I'll let you handle the night watch. I need to get some rest also and make sure my camp is peaceful." The Colonel said.

CHAPTER ELEVEN

The morning rolled in and Joe was ready for the day. He met with the Marshal for breakfast and they sat talking about normal things. Anyone seeing them would think they were just starting another normal day. Actually Joe was excited about this coming day. He could see that things probably would be turned over in a short time. There was no danger as far as he could see since no one could have been planning this event. The world was almost looking rosy again. The only catch would be if a person managed to sneak past the cavalry and get to Bisbee.

After the two men had eaten they walked to the Marshal's office as they normally did. The Colonel was to meet them there and they would start operations then. The Marshal had obtained the agreement of a minister to use the basement of his church for holding prisoners temporarily. He was not let in on the operation but the Marshal felt he was trustworthy. Joe and the Marshal sat in his office waiting for the Colonel and they scanned the local map. There were about ten country living people that would be taken also. The others were all town residents. The banker here was one. This could cause some problems with the possibility of a run on the place. Such was part of the dangers.

The Colonel arrived and he sat down with them for a short time. He had sent men down to Bisbee to camp out of town. He also had put men out to ride the city limits to stop anyone from leaving once the plan was in operation. He had a squad here at the Marshal's office to be ready for anything if needed. Things were set so the plan began. The three men walked to stores to start things. There were about five business people involved so they were taken out first. The first arrested were not involved with any resistance. Most were changed into shells of disbelief and sad acceptance. It took about three hours to clean the town up and by now innocent people were beginning to see what was happening. The prisoners were placed in the church basement and a squad of cavalry was set as guards.

Now the three headed out in the country. A squad of soldiers was along with them. The longest time needed involved the distance from town the target persons were. Another three hours were taken to grab these people. The ten people were tied on their horses and everyone headed back to town. Now the lawmen had a larger group to keep control of. The squad of soldiers was sufficient to hold these prisoners. The Colonel, Joe and the Marshal now sat down in the office. They had a couple of very stiff drinks there and felt good about the days work. They would head off to Bisbee in the morning. The soldiers here were to stay here. The Marshal agreed to swear in a sergeant as a temporary deputy to keep the town under control while he was gone. In turn, the Marshal was deputized under Joe. Everything had to be maintained honestly. This day's work was finished. Joe had to send a telegram to his office and they needed to figure where these people would be tried.

CHAPTER ELEVEN

The Marshal and Joe walked the Main Street in the afternoon to give out information as required. Many people had not known about the sedition plans. A few did but were not involved. Most residents now were glad the plan had been stopped. Finally everything was almost back to normal. The three men now sat in a saloon and watched the residents. This was a place where input could be gained just by watching the various customers. Besides being almost a requirement, the men were enjoying their rest and drink.

A few residents actually came up to the three men and thanked them for doing their duty. The conclusion of the plan here had worked well. Now they could only hope that Bisbee might be as easy. The telegraph became operational now and only messages to Bisbee and Douglas were held up. Headquarters sent Joe a big congratulations and the Colonel's command had sent a similar note. It was almost relaxing to sit here knowing that things were finished here and shortly should be completed to the south.

Around 7 this evening a telegraph came to the Colonel from his troop down by Bisbee. The Mexican Army had set up a large camp just across the border. Now the Colonel was very concerned. These Mexican soldiers might just be waiting until a take over had started there. He wired back to his group and ordered them to set up camp directly across from the Mexican military. They might have to go head to head with them if anything started. Things must have been about ready to spring out down there. The three men here now made some rapid plans. They needed to get moving and head off trouble before it got started. They all agreed to head down to Bisbee this night. They gathered what they needed and the Colonel took half the soldiers left here to ride with him. This would bring a larger force to confront the Mexican Army if needed.

The group headed off and hoped to be in Bisbee tomorrow morning. They wanted to get there and clean things up.

"Guess we might have settled down too soon." Joe said.

"Yup, maybe we should have not been celebrating and moving instead." The Colonel said.

"I think we can still handle things if we act fast now. Joe said.

The two towns had to be tied up as soon as possible. The Colonel was very concerned about the Mexican Army being at the border. The take over must have been planned to occur very soon.

"I think this is called counting your chickens before......" Joe said.

The group rode steady and did not over push the horses. They needed to stay in shape for the entire ride. The night was very nice and with stars and moon out a person could see very well. The group made good time and just after sunrise they were gaining the outskirts of Bisbee. The Colonel decided to ride directly to his men's camp along the border. This not only would be a show of force but also get everyone into the town area. Later they could decide how to begin this operation. The Colonel accomplished what he wanted as he rode into this camp. The Mexican command saw immediately what was going on. They doubled their border posts to be ready if the cavalry made a confrontation.

A quick check with the junior officers here and the Colonel learned that no indication of a coming show down had been seen. The local people did not seem overly worried about why the cavalry was here. The Colonel now sat down with Joe and the Marshal to begin plans for the clean up. As with Tombstone, a guard had to be placed on the way toward Douglas. Two hours after they had arrived in Bisbee the operation began. Twenty top leaders were apprehended and kept under guard until Joe could find a useable place to hold them. Three hours was all that was required for the arrest of all known people involved in the insurrection.

CHAPTER ELEVEN

Joe got busy and found a holding place. He managed to find the City Hall, which had a large basement. This would work for now. Now the mission had to move to Douglas. This was a place that Joe was concerned about. His recent contact with lawmen there had not been comfortable. They evidently were involved with the leaders there. The Colonel's junior officers had been watching the Mexican Army personnel and it was plain they were getting nervous. As the time ticked away, it became a question if the Mexican men would jump the border and start into a battle with the cavalry. The Colonel ordered his men to be on a high alert and expect such activity.

Now the three men with twenty cavalry headed off to Douglas. This would be the final leg of this operation. Everyone hoped things would go easy without a hard fight. The group rode into Douglas by late afternoon. Things had to be finished this day. Anything left undone would leave an avenue that anyone could use to begin operations again. The group initially went to the town Marshal's officer. Joe immediately greeted the men here and asked straight out if they were involved in the movement to change governments. All but one man admitted they were in favor of this. Joe advised they were under arrest at this point and took their weapons. They were placed in a cell within the town jail for now. Now the three men began grabbing everyone they had information on and holding them. Two hours of hard and fast work finally brought the town under new management. The arrested residents were placed in the hold area under the town hall. Now a few country residents had to be secured. The military men were sent out to the various ranches known to be in favor of the government change. After four hours, Douglas was finished. Soldiers were left as guards and the three men rode back to Bisbee. Joe was glad he had investigated everyone around these two towns before. This allowed the entire operation to be finished and the captives were generally admitting they had been involved with the attempt to bring back the Mexican Government.

The Colonel now went up to the camp at the border and he talked with his men for a while. Finally he walked to the border and called for the Mexican Commander. A man stepped up and introduced himself as a major in command. The Colonel advised the major about the actions on the states side. He also asked if the army would now retreat since their presence was no longer able to accomplish the take over. The major agreed with the Colonel and they would be leaving in the morning. The Colonel maintained his camp here in case the Mexican Army tried to ease over the border during the night. Several large fires were built and maintained through the night.

As the evening grew and three men now settled down to relax. The deputy that had been made Sheriff after the old one was killed came to the three and they invited him to join them with some drink. The talk now would be geared to make sure this man was agreeable to this operation and would stand behind what had been accomplished

CHAPTER TWELVE

Morning found the Mexican Army packing up to retreat. This was a good sign and now things began to look good here. The Colonel was happy and his superiors would be also. Joe sent a telegraph back to Prescott and his job here was basically finished. He hoped there was no new assignment that needed immediate attention. He planned to return to Tombstone and enjoy the luxuries there, including the Birdcage hospitality. Prescott wired back to Joe and advised the prisoners would have to be moved to Tucson over the next week. The cavalry would be asked to escort the prisoners and later a trial would be set up. The prisoners numbered about fifty and this would require at least two rail cars to transport them. The Colonel offered to maintain the prisoners in the three towns until their shipment could be arranged. This was great for Joe and the Marshal as they could get back to Tombstone. They would leave in the morning. This last day would be used to clean up their operations and secure the evidence on these criminals.

Assignments were figured out and given to various soldiers. Such things were simple and only required some time to obtain what information was needed for evidence. The soldiers actually were enjoying this change to their routine. Many were volunteering to do things. The Colonel was very proud of his men and this was showing now. By late evening most things had been secured. What little was left could be obtained by soldiers that would be staying here as guards for the prisoners. The evening came and this would be the last time for all the four men to be together for a while. The new Sheriff at Bisbee was enjoying his position and his power had grown much larger with this operation.

Many of the prisoners were demanding an attorney. Joe advised them he needed a note and location for any attorney that could be reached. He did mention that the Territory would not fund any of these attorneys so the individual would have to fund this. Most of the prisoners were figuring that charges either would be dropped or would be scaled down on them. This was the common thought of the men. Now Joe advised they needed to be aware that they would all face murder charges in addition to the other charges. The murder charge was added since people had been killed over the last two weeks. This was a sobering towel to the prisoners now. They began seeing that this operation was not a slipshod legal thing.

The last evening was passed with enjoyment by the lawmen and the Colonel. They drank a lot of good whiskey and agreed to meet again at a later time. They had all become friends over this operation. Joe sat up until almost ten, which was very unusual for him. He would only have to ride back to Tombstone in the morning so he didn't care what he might feel like then.

The sun rose and greeted Joe. He dressed and walked to the café for his breakfast. He met the Marshal and the Sheriff there. The Colonel had eaten with his men today. He was staying in Bisbee for a few days and then he would return

CHAPTER TWELVE

to Camp Huachuca. After breakfast Joe and the Marshal headed off. The soldiers here along with the local lawmen would have no trouble with the prisoners. The Mexican authority had been deflated and moved back to the south. Joe had good thoughts about his coming rewards for this night. He saw the Marshal smiling to himself at times and figured he was thinking of similar rewards. He was not married but had a couple of lady friends. He had never figured he was a very good catch as he might be killed at anytime. The ladies did not seem to worry about this however. Each one tried to out do the other one.

The trail was not busy this day. Joe wondered if this might be from information about what was going around here. The whole thing was finished now except the trials. As Joe kept watch he noticed a small group of men riding with about twenty five head of cattle to the east. This seemed a little odd to him since there were no known ranches around here yet. He mentioned this to the Marshal and they sat for a few minutes talking. Both men now agreed this might be checked out in case something fishy was going on.

The rode toward the men and the men stopped as they came close.

"What's happening?" Joe asked.

"Not much, just moving these cattle that got out of their range." One man said.

"What ranch do you work around here?" Joe asked. "I didn't think there were any working ranches in this area."

There was a pause now as the men sought something to help them. The men could gather nothing.

"Where do you fellows live?" Joe asked.

"Just at the ranch, no where else." A man stated.

"Well, just where is your ranch then? Can't see anything around here." Joe stated.

"It looks that these cattle are range kept and basically belong to the Indians around here." Joe said. "I sure wouldn't be wanting to steal anything from them. I hear they actually still skin men alive."

This hit the men as both lawmen could see. The men looked at each other and then one man asked. "If we turn these loose here would that be ok?"

"Should be, but I can't say what the Indian braves might think." Joe said. "You might want to ride away fairly fast. Those silhouettes you can see are not white men."

The men were very nervous now. The lawmen were enjoying all this.

"We really didn't mean anything by rounding up these critters. We thought they were available to anyone that found them." A man stated.

"The rule here is any cattle found out on the range belong to the Indians. They are very strong with this rule." Joe said. "I think I'd head off and ride hard toward Bisbee if I was you."

"Yes sir. We will do that. And Thanks!" A man said as they group turned and headed to the south. They dug into their horses now and were making a hard run. Joe didn't think the Indians would worry now.

"Seems someone is always anxious to claim range beef. This is where the Indians get bad attitudes toward the average white man." Joe stated as he and the Marshal turned back toward the trail.

They had ridden about three miles when a group of braves came riding up. The Marshal was concerned but Joe wasn't.

"Don't worry about those braves. They just want to thank us for saving their cattle." Joe told him.

The braves rode up and gave Joe a sweeping hand as a thank you. Joe returned the gesture.

"White war chief help us again. White war chief very good man. He never have problems around us. We celebrate at full moon if white war chief come to camp." The leader of the group spoke.

CHAPTER TWELVE

"Thank you Many Moons. I will come if I can." Joe told them. They gave a gesture again and turned to ride off. Joe sat there a minute and the Marshal as sitting with many questions.

"You know those Indians?" He asked.

"Yup. Seen them many times and they always seem to observe me whatever I am doing. In fact they had saved my hide a lot of times. Joe told him "Guess we best get moving again."

The two turned back on the trail and continued on to Tombstone. The ride on seemed to be shorter now. Joe was pleased that he was able to do something for the Indians again. He was smiling as he rode into town with the Marshal.

The town appeared to be fairly quiet this afternoon. The two lawmen rode to the Marshal's office and stepped inside. They needed to see how things had been going since the operation took down of some of the citizens here. There wasn't much for information and from deputy reports the town had been quiet since the Marshal had left. This was some good information to the Marshal and Joe. They stepped over to the saloon for a couple of drinks after their long ride. Joe felt very good now and he was toying with the idea of more relaxation over at the Birdcage. He figured to get a good meal first and the Marshal was all for this also.

As the two lawmen walked down the street local residents would speak and nod to them. It looked as if the population here had appreciated the late raids. Joe was hoping for similar results down in Bisbee and Douglas. They entered a café that they knew served good food and ordered a big steak. The two were busy in their meal when a person ran into the café.

"Jack Lane is over at the Birdcage and shooting up the place as well as some rough play." The man hollered.

Both lawmen jumped up and hit the street on the run. Jack Lane was a known hoodlum around here. He always seemed to be in a trouble spot as he picked on the civilized population. The Marshal hoped the place was not very busy and there might not be a chance of someone getting hurt. So far Lane had not killed anyone but he inflicted many serious injuries.

The lawmen hit the door of the Birdcage and barged inside. Lane was standing at the bar with a drink in his hands. He saw from the mirror against the bar wall that the lawmen had arrived. He smiled and turned slowly around.

"Howdy men. Suppose you came to tame me down." Lane said.

"That's true and to add things I think you will spend at least a night in jail. The Marshal told him.

"Can't do that Marshal. I still haven't caught up on my whiskey here." Lane said.

"Well I suppose we can handle this the hard way." The Marshal said as he pulled his gun.

"Don't even think about reaching for your iron. I won't hesitate a second to kill you!" The Marshal said.

Lane looked around the room and he seemed to be gauging if he could make it to his gun or not. He smiled now and turned around to pour himself another drink. The Marshal was not ready to play games now. He fired his Colt and blew the glass out of Lane's hand. Now Lane was mad. He turned straight around and looked the Marshal in the eye.

"Guess you don't want to play anymore............" Lane said as he reached for his pistol. Another bark spoke out from the Marshal's gun and Lane looked funny at the man.

"You.......... " He said as he slumped toward the floor. The thud was heard plain and some people close came up. Some one said to get the doctor but the Marshal stopped that. He knew that Lane was dead.

"Ok, everyone back off and get your business going. This is not a side show." The Marshal said.

He called for two men to carry Lane to the undertakers and he nodded to Joe. They walked outside the

CHAPTER TWELVE

door. There were some people starting to gather here now. Things like this did not happen often anymore. The lawmen knew that such things would continue to happen and there was only them to stop such things and keep them away from the residents.

A WASTELAND OF OUTLAWS

CHAPTER THIRTEEN

Joe had passed the night as he had planned and now he was waiting to see if Headquarters might have a new assignment for him. He wanted to stop by Camp Huachuca but the Colonel wouldn't be there for a couple of days yet. He would have to wait on everyone again.

He didn't mind since he was in Tombstone. The town was quiet this day and no mention was made about the problem last night. Joe now planned on riding out and circle the town some to check on possible problems coming. He seemed at ease but he was worried about how things might be with families of the arrested men living in the country. Such people never gave thought to what might happen with their families if they were caught. Many families had to scrape by and at times they could be left to starve. Many saloon girls ended up from situations like this.

Joe was enjoying his ride and it seemed that Jean was also. She generally loved to be moving and not penned up in a stable. Joe rode around some of the ranches that had been hurt by the operation. The families were all still there and they seemed to be getting along for now. Many times neighbors would step in and help the families. Some of these men might not get out of prison for many years. Joe did notice that there were For Sale signs at the front gates of a couple of ranches. Evidently the families were planning to move somewhere else and try to get out of the picture of what their men had done. Joe always wondered if people caught in problems might head back east or on to California.

The day moved on and soon Joe was riding to the north of Tombstone. He noticed the sun was hanging around 1 in the afternoon. His ears suddenly heard some shots being fired off to his left. He spurred Jean on and soon was within sight of the problem. The stage was running toward Tombstone and a couple of bandits were chasing it. Joe clicked into high gear and he could see that the bandits had not noticed him as yet. He rode hard and gained a position behind the two men. Now he drew his Colt and began speaking to these men. They immediately saw they had a problem and both turned off the trail of the stage and were riding hard. Joe was right on them and he ran them about a mile. Their horses were getting winded it appeared and he was able to shoot one man off his horse. He gained on the last man now and came along side of him. He hit the man with a short whip he carried for this purpose and the man fell to the ground. Joe had heard of men jumping another man from a horse. A person could get hurt doing stunts like this. Joe reined in and checked the man on the ground. He was basically out for now and Joe tied him up. He would put the man on his horse when he came around.

Joe left the man on the ground tied up and mounted Jean to check on the second man. He covered the distance in a short time and found this man was no longer available here. He tied this man on his horse and rode back to the other man. Here he noticed the man was gaining consciousness. He helped the man on his horse and tied him there also. Now he would ride back to Tombstone to deliver both men. He

CHAPTER THIRTEEN

thought these men were not overly smart and probably had never done much as bandits. Joe walked Jean and the other horses along to give them a rest from the hard chase. The bandits horses were very winded and they wouldn't be much good for a while.

Joe and the bandits rode into town and he headed straight for the jail. He deposited the one man here and then took the other to the undertaker. He finished all this and sat down in the Marshal's office. He had his day filled now and was glad he had not been injured. He would allow Tombstone to handle the trial of the one man still alive. If the man drew prison time then he would be sent to Yuma. The Marshal had received word that a train to handle the other prisoners would be coming by tomorrow. This would free up all the space being used to hold these men. Their trial would be announced later. Joe knew he had to go to Tucson for this. He really never cared for Tucson and managed to stay clear of the town most of the time. They did have some good lawmen there so he never was concerned about this.

Joe walked to a saloon and took a table to watch the residents as they came in. Things seemed very normal here and he actually was enjoying the late afternoon. He wasn't sure if everything had been blown over and buried from the operation but things seemed like this. The Marshal walked in the saloon later and saw Joe. He came straight over to the table and took a seat.

"Well how are things with you this afternoon? Haven't hardly moved since I left you, right?" Joe said.

"Sure, you can afford to be lazy since you don't have to please any of the population." The Marshal replied.

"I was thinking about going over to the Birdcage later and find a nice cheap card game. Haven't played cards in a while." Joe said. "I might even figure to retire here on my winnings. That should scare you a bunch!"

The Marshal frowned at Joe and shook his head.

"Well I'm sure you can find something over there. I don't recommend the basement since they have some very expensive games down there." The Marshal said.

"So did you get things organized for the trial of the bandit I brought in today?" Joe asked.

"Yup. Should be handled tomorrow if that's all right with you. The Judge knew you needed to be freed as soon as possible." The Marshal said.

"Great. Then I will have to find out about Tucson and the big trial there. Will you be able to go there also? I think your testimony will be required also." Joe said.

"Expect so." The Marshal replied.

The two men sat for a couple of drinks then they walked to the café for super. They had a good meal and then Joe walked to the Birdcage. The Marshal had more things to do yet. Joe walked in the Birdcage door and some people saw him. Things got very quiet for a minute. Joe smiled at everyone and slowly things went back to normal. Joe walked to the back of the stage where some games were being played. He asked about bets and found a cheap table for him to play at. The men here were probably miners or cowboys off for the night. They generally didn't have much money. This was fine with Joe. He didn't usually win much but the games were a relaxing mode for him.

"Have you guys finished with your mess?" A man asked Joe.

"Yeah basically anyway. Only trials left." Joe told them. He did not worry about these men since most could care less who was running the area.

"We're playing dealers choice. You can play and then drop out whenever you need to." A man stated.

"Sounds good to me. How much for the ante?" Joe asked.

"Nothing very much. Usually a quarter will do it." A man replied. "Sometimes bets get a little higher but that usually drops the person doing the raises."

CHAPTER THIRTEEN

Joe sat and played for a couple hours. He lost about $3 for the evening. He thanked the men and closed out. He decided not to partake of any other things available here. He walked back outside and sat on a bench in front of the Marshal's office. He was enjoying the cool of the evening and kept an eye out for the Marshal. The man should be out doing a patrol. Things were very quiet and this was peaceful for lawmen. A person still had to kept alert but overall things were doing well.

Joe sat on his bench for about 30 minutes and the Marshal walked up.

"It took you long enough to get back here. I could have died of thirst while waiting for you." Joe told him.

"Well you look as if you are still ok. I suppose what you said was a hint you are ready for a drink." The Marshal replied.

The two men walked toward a saloon. There had been no talk about the stage robbery earlier. Joe expected most people only wanted to relax after all the excitement around here of late. The customers in the saloon were the normal ones and these hardly ever got into a round of fists. Joe was tired after everything this day so he didn't want to stay up late. They had a couple of drinks and then Joe bid the Marshal a goodnight. They would get together for breakfast.

The next day started normally and after breakfast Joe walked to the livery to check on Jean. He had ordered a brushing and some oats for her after yesterday. She always was ready when he needed her. The Marshal had advised Joe that court would start at 10. So Joe was ready for all this. He stopped by the telegraph office and found a message from headquarters. They wanted him to head for Tucson as soon as things here were over. The trial in Tucson would probably roll over a week. Joe didn't care much for Tucson but he knew he had to be there for the trial.

Court time was short and the robber had been found guilty. The Judge sentenced the man to Yuma for 15 years.

A WASTELAND OF OUTLAWS

This was a little strange since normally anyone involved in a crime where someone was killed was hanged. Joe didn't care one way or the other. The man would be held until a wagon came through and then he would be hauled to Benson to get the train on to Yuma. Trains were becoming a very neat thing around since they cut travel time. Joe had heard that the run from Tucson to Yuma was a nasty thing however. For every train that traveled this line, two had to run with water and wood for it. The railroads were in the process of getting coal shipped in from Pennsylvania back east. They could run twice as far with this fuel.

CHAPTER FOURTEEN

Joe had finished up everything in Tombstone now so he headed off toward Tucson. He did like the ride since it gave him the freedom that he and Jean loved so much. The trip would take about three days and he had obtained some trail rations for the trip. He always made sure he had something to eat. A person could never tell when they might get into a problem and not able to move fast.

The day was very nice and no threat of storms or wind had been seen. Joe rode along and kept an eye out. He always watched for things that most people would never see. The day wore on and in late afternoon Joe saw an old cabin that had always been vacant. This time he saw smoke coming from the stovepipe on the roof. This was different so he rode toward the cabin. He managed to get fairly close without giving anyone a warning. Now he walked up to the side of the place.

"HELLO in the cabin. Whose in there?" Joe hollered.

A WASTELAND OF OUTLAWS

A voice answering asked. "Who wants to know?"

"Arizona Ranger. Step outside with your hand up and no guns." Joe told them.

There was a pause and then the door opened slowly. Joe was ready for anything now. The door opened enough for a person to get out and a man came walking carefully through it. He had his hands up and was wearing no gun belt.

"Anyone else in the cabin besides you?" Joe asked.

"Yes, my wife. We are new here and just found this place abandon so figured we could use it." The man said.

The woman now walked outside and looked at Joe. Both these people were definitely of the farmer type. They didn't have much for clothing as theirs were well worn. They made a picture of sorry circumstances. Joe had seen this many times and it always was sad. People like this got down on their luck and lived in misery. Joe talked with the couple for a few minutes and then walked to his horse.

"I have to get moving. A lot of daylight left yet. You two take care now." Joe told them as he flipped a double eagle at them. He was more than glad to help if they would use this for getting some badly needed items. Joe wheeled Jean around and rode off.

Joe wondered if people like this would ever move ahead and get to where life could be enjoyable. Most he had seen never did. They seemed to be set into a mold that would never allow them any freedom from their poverty. Joe rode to a campsite he knew about ten miles from this cabin. He would spend the night here and enjoy the clear night with stars shining just for him.

The rest of the ride to Tucson was normal and he had only seen a couple other men during this stretch of the trail. He rode into Tucson and stopped by the Sheriff's office. Sam was the Sheriff here and a good man. He also had five deputies that enabled him to control crime around the town. The two men sat and talked for a short time then Joe headed

CHAPTER FOURTEEN

to get a room for the night. He told Sam he would catch him later. He obtained a room and then took Jean around back. This hotel had a small livery out behind it for customer's animals. The boy running the place knew Joe so he would take good care of Jean.

Joe walked to a café and had a good meal. Now he decided to get a drink. He knew most places here and was not thrilled by many of them. He went to a place he knew and found it was about the same. Customers inside did not pay any attention to him as he entered. The bartender set a bottle and glass in front of him and Joe poured the drink. There were about ten people here and all seemed to be normal local residents just in for a short time to have one or two drinks. Joe stood at the bar and watched things. He was glad he had never become a bartender since he knew he could not handle his cool with some of the attitudes of customers.

A man came in from the street and looked around. He walked to the bar and loudly called the bartender.

"Heh old man. I need a drink and fast." The man said.

The bartender looked at the man and nodded. He was pouring a drink for another man and evidently this was not acceptable to the new man.

"I SAID I WANT A DRINK!" The new man shouted.

"I'll be with you in a second. Hold your horse." The bartender told the man.

The new man slammed his fist down on the bar and grabbed a beer mug. He threw the mug and hit the bartender on the side of his head. The man almost dropped but managed to hang onto the bar for support.

"Now I want that drink!" The new man said.

Joe now became involved. "The man asked for a second. Now I think you need to move along and hope you can get a drink at another place."

"This ain't any of your business." The new man said.

"Well it is now. I'm a Ranger and you have just ran out of luck." Joe told him.

The man looked at Joe and everyone could see he had not noticed the Ranger before. The man lifted an eyebrow and looked at Joe as if he was trying to decide what to do. Finally the man turned and walked out of the door. The bartender was getting back his feet and he thanked Joe. The mug had brought a knot on the man's head but he refused to go to the doctor. He had been given things like this in the past.

Joe had two more drinks and then decided it was time to head for his room. He needed some rest and then he could start out in the morning with the coming trial. Joe thanked the bartender and walked outside. The street was still light and there were some people walking along the boardwalks. Joe looked around as was his normal procedure coming out of the building.

"Heh lawman. You still bothering innocent citizens?" A man's voice said.

Joe looked in the direction the voice came from and saw the man standing partly in the street. It was the man from the incident in the saloon. The man was watching carefully as Joe turned. He crouched into a gunfighter's stance now and seemed to be waiting for Joe to do something.

"What's your beef?" Joe asked.

"I just don't like lawmen. You are always stopping things that don't involve you." The man said.

Joe squared up in front of the man. The two men stood silent and staring at each other for a few seconds. Each second drew by with the speed of a snail. Joe was waiting for the man to make his move. He knew it was coming but a person had to be very alert as it could start at any time. The street had grown very still and no sounds could be heard anywhere as the seconds ticked on. Joe was watching the man's face very carefully. Men usually made a slight movement in the their jaw just before they reached for their

CHAPTER FOURTEEN

pistol. Joe did not say a thing and the other man was quiet also.

Joe was wondered if the man was turning down from this showdown. There was nothing that Joe could see for this delay. Next Joe saw the twitch that gave the sign. The man suddenly grabbed for his gun and a Colt spoke. The man stopped with his hand on his gun and stared at Joe. Joe's Colt was smoking and he watched the man. There was no movement at all. Joe was concerned that he might have missed the man. In the hour of seconds now the man took a step forward. He turned and fell on his back. No other movement was seen. Joe carefully edged toward the man not sure if he was faking or really dead. When Joe reached the man there was no movement and Joe could see the man was not breathing. He accepted this as proof the man was gone.

Sam came running up at this time and saw what had occurred. He checked the man over and looked at Joe.

"I believe you dodged death once again, Joe." The Sheriff told Joe.

"I wasn't looking for a fight but I didn't want to die either." Joe said.

"You know, I think this cuss was wanted. Have to check that out back at the office." Sam said.

Sam told a couple of men standing around to carry the body to the undertakers. Next he talked with some witness's and got the story. He already knew that Joe was totally in the right and things like this happened every once and a while. Always some stupid man with a chip had to start things. Now things were quiet again so he and Sam entered the saloon and had a couple drinks to settle the shakes. After everything now Joe again decided to try for some rest.

A WASTELAND OF OUTLAWS

CHAPTER FIFTEEN

The next morning arrived with freshness. Joe took care of his morning chores and then walked to the Sheriff's office. Today he needed to find out about the court trial and how long it might be. Sam and Joe walked to the Judge's office and he invited them in. They discussed things a few minutes and then the Judge told them they would begin things in the morning. A couple of men had not arrived yet but that could be handled when they did arrive. The lawmen thanked the Judge and left. They split up now as Sam had some things to do and Joe needed to check on Jean. He felt safe for her since the boy at the livery always had liked her.

Joe decided to get his gun checked now since this town had one of the best gunsmith's known. He always could use more ammo also. He handed the gunsmith his pistol and he would standby while the man checked everything about it. Meanwhile Joe looked through the man's pistols. He had some very nice ones but nothing like his own. The gunsmith was also very aware of the Ranger's pistol. He still called it a

Colt but it was far ahead of that. Everything was in good shape with Joe's pistol so the gunsmith handed it back. Joe reloaded the gun and put it in his holster ready for use.

Joe bought some ammo and walked back on the street. He would put the ammo in his room for now. He walked down the street and saw nothing of importance to him. He sat down on a bench and watched the people scurrying about. Finally he saw Sam and watched as he was talking with a cowboy that had just ridden into town. They talked for a few minutes and the man was using a lot of hand motions as if he was telling Sam about something. The cowboy left and headed back out of town. Sam walked to Joe and sat down.

"You looking for something to do?" He asked Joe.

"Either way. You must have something to do since you asked that question." Joe stated.

"Yup, that cowboy told me of a body outside town about four miles. I need to go check it out." Sam said.

"Ok with me. I'll get my horse." Joe said as he stood up. He walked to the livery and saddled Jean then walked to the Sheriff's Office. Sam was standing by his horse in front and waiting for Joe. He saw Joe and stepped up on his horse. Joe mounted also. The two rode off to the west out of town. Sam knew the area of course and had been surprised that a person could have been picked off out here. There was nothing around except a lonely cactus at times and some very small scrub brush.

"Sure ain't much out here to hide behind. Don't know if this was a mutual gunfight or if it was a bushwhacking." Sam said.

"Never can tell at times. Over there." Joe said pointing to the left. "That looks like a body.'

"Yup. Let's see what we find." Sam replied as he turned his horse toward the body.

The two men rode up and dismounted. The body was not dead too long as it wasn't stiff yet. Sam checked things over and found a bullet hole through the man's chest. He searched the man for any identification but found nothing. The man did have $25 on him. This was not a robbery. A horse was not seen anywhere near. This was different as most killings left the horse because of the ease of identification by local people. If a killer rode into town with a horse that belonged to someone else there would be a question. This was becoming a strange case now. Sam did not recognize this man and he appeared to be a cowhand by his clothes.

Joe started walking around the area and looking at the ground for any signs it might show. He found hoof prints that showed the man had been walking. Boot prints came to the sight and none left. This man either didn't have a horse or the killer had stolen it. One of them had been on foot. There was not much evidence about this killing so far. The ground was showing that the rider and the horse had ridden up to the man walking and they had met. Things looked a little as if the two men had both been on the ground for a short time. The tracks of the dead man showed him standing and then falling, probably from being shot. The boot tracks were the same from both men. The normal for around here was showing nothing but smooth soles.

Finally Sam had seen enough. "Let's head back and I'll send the undertaker out to get the body. Can't find much else here."

"I think I would like to follow the boot tracks back a ways and see what might show up." Joe said.

"Well, ok. I'm out of my territory anyway. I'll see you when you get back." Sam told him.

Both men now headed off in opposite directions. Joe had a fairly easy trail following the boot tracks backwards. The man must have been fairly heavy as shown by his tracks. This was something that Joe had not noticed back at the site of the killing. Joe followed the tracks for another four miles and then a couple of men came riding up to him. These men were not cowhands by the look of their clothing.

"Howdy Ranger. You seen a man walking up ahead?" One of the men asked.

"Yes but not walking. He was dead." Joe told them.

"Well looks like our man might not have made it very far. He had just robbed us at our mine up there." The man said as he pointed up toward a small rise.

"Where did you take the man?" The other man asked.

"No where yet. The Sheriff was heading back to town to get the undertaker. You say the man robbed you?" Joe asked.

"Sure as Hell did. Came right in and held us up." The first man said. "The guy worked for us about two months."

"Well let's ride back then and have you look at the dead man." Joe said.

The three men turned and rode back toward the killing spot. The two men were co-owners of the mine. They had found it about five years ago and it was worth working. They had been getting about four ounces of gold a month from the mine. They had hired the new man to help them get more product out of the mine. He had been a good worker but must have decided to get more than wages. The three men rode up to the body and the two mine men immediately told Joe that this man was not the right one. Now things were beginning to make more sense to Joe. Evidently the man that had robbed the mine was walking. He found a man on a horse and had shot the man and stole his horse. The gold probably was getting very heavy by this time. This might explain the heavier boot prints also. Joe got a description from the mine men and then rode back to town.

Joe rode up to Sam's office and told him about the information he had gained. This was a pleasant ending for now. He thought as Joe was telling him of the description of the man. No one close to that as far as he knew. He might never have been around this town. They at least had the information about what had happened. The man probably never came close to Tucson after all this. The dead man might not be known around here also. There were a lot of drifters flowing through area anymore.

It took the undertaker two hours to get the body and return to town. He had seen this man but had no idea who he was. Sam had looked through his wanted posters when he first returned to town but had not found him. Sam needed to find out who this man was if at all possible. It never seemed right for a man to meet his maker and having no one know who he was. Sam suggested they walk to the saloon and ask some regular customers to look at the man. So the two lawmen headed off on their official quest and they would combine some imbibing of favorite drink also.

In the second saloon the bartender pointed a man out to the lawmen. This guy had been waiting here for a few hours hoping to meet up with a friend that was suppose to be here. The two walked over to the man and talked with him for a short time. After this the three men walked outside and over to the undertakers. This man would know if the dead man was who he was looking for. They walked into the undertakers place and the owner showed them where the body was.

The three men walked into the room and the Sheriff opened the box. The man from the saloon looked and shook his head. This was his friend but who would do this to the man. The lawmen were pleased that dead man had been drawn back to the world of knowledge about him. He, at the least, would not go to his reward without anyone knowing who he was. The Sheriff thanked the man for helping them. He walked out and the lawmen talked with the undertaker for a few minutes. The man would be buried tomorrow.

Things had been figured out now and the only thing the lawmen didn't know was the actual purpose of the killing. They walked to the Sheriff's office and sat down to think things over. A boy from the telegraph office came in and handed the Sheriff a telegram. It was from the Marshal at Florence. He had a run in with a man earlier this day and was checking if anyone knew the person or had any problems with gold. This man had rode into Florence and was trying to sell some gold to the bank. The banker had managed to contact the Marshal and when he arrived at the bank, the man with the gold got into a shouting match with the banker and the Marshal. He had finally reached for his gun and the Marshal had to shoot him. Now Joe and Sam began seeing that this was probably their man. Sam went to the telegraph office and sent a wire back asking about the horse. When the response came back, the horse was described along with the man and things fit in place. This case was closed but unfortunately all those involved were dead. The mine owners would be pleased that their property had been found.

CHAPTER SIXTEEN

As morning was born, Joe was anxious to get moving and help the trial get into motion. He had researched his mental knowledge of everything that would be important for the trial. There would be no hold ups because of him. He sat in the Sheriff's office after breakfast and both of them waited for the time to come around. Finally it was getting close to ten and the two lawmen headed toward the court. The trial had been broadcast to many people and the Territory was hoping to end any future problems along this line as well as take care of the current problem. Many people had traveled to Tucson just for the trial and Joe hoped things did not get out of hand. He and Sam had talked about this and were prepared for whatever might come.

The Marshal from Tombstone had arrived late last night and now the law was ready. The prosecutor had discussed the case with them and they knew what he wanted to present. The program was about to start. Everyone hoped the trial was not stretched out and things moved rapidly. The prisoners of course felt different. The charges for some of the prisoners included murder charges. If they were found guilty then a hanging would probably be required.

The Judge entered the courtroom at ten and things started. The prosecutor started with the Marshal and then Joe. They were the main menu for the prosecution. Other men would be called after this to incase the activity that had occurred in Bisbee, Douglas and Tombstone. The court adjourned at 1 in the afternoon for lunch. Testimony was almost used up for now. After the lunch period, court was called to order and a witness remaining for the prosecutor was called. The prosecution was finished and the trail was handed over to the defense. The attorney handling the defense did not appear to be interested in the case and was only doing the motions for a defense. The trail was closed about 3 and turned over to the jury. The jury returned to the court in 30 minutes and gave the Judge their verdict of Guilty. The Judge adjourned the court and advised he would handle the sentences in the morning.

The lawmen walked outside the court and they agreed to head for the saloon. Sam had to check with his office first in case there was anything important for him there. Joe and the Marshal from Tombstone walked to the saloon and found an empty table. The bartender brought a bottle and glasses. The pressing day had passed and now Joe was sure he would be free to head back into his territory. Sam walked in the saloon and found the other two men. He had nothing at the office except Joe's headquarters wanted him to wire as soon as the trial was over. They must have something hot coming up.

"I don't know why you can't just tell your highers where to go." Sam said.

"That would be fine until I needed some money. Can't get that stuff from goofing around very long." Joe replied. "If you have need for a hanging on these prisoners do you think you might need me?"

CHAPTER SIXTEEN

"Well I could say yes as you probably hope, but actually we have things like that under control. Your headquarters knows this of course." Sam said.

"Thanks for nothing Sam." Joe said smiling.

The lawmen sat in the saloon for about an hour then they split up to go to their individual places. Joe walked to the livery and checked on Jean. She was being taken care of very nicely. He stretched and headed for his room. It might be nice to get a nights sleep here. He entered his room and looked out the window to the street below. Just at that time four men came riding hard down the street. This did not seem right to Joe and he was glued to the window for now. The four pulled up by the saloon and dismounted, running into the saloon. Joe figured they must have been cowhands in a hurry to get a drink. For some reason however, Joe stood at the window.

Things were quiet for about 10 minutes, and then the four men came back out of the saloon and headed toward the Sheriff's office. They were walking fairly fast but in a determined way. Joe watched from his viewpoint and wondered what they might be up to. At this point Joe grabbed his hat and headed out. He walked out of the hotel and looked toward the Sheriff's office. There was no movement around there now. He was alarmed about this so he trotted toward the office. Upon arrival at the office, he could hear loud voices from inside. The four men were arguing with Sam. Joe approached the door and eased it open. The four men were in a stance that Joe considered dangerous. They were acting more like gun hands now. The four were to the side and in front of Joe so he walked in without much fanfare. Sam was relieved to see him as Joe could see on his face. Joe had drawn his Colt ready for action. One man had glanced at Joe and was about to say something when another man reached for his gun. This man stopped living fast. Now the other three knew that Joe was behind them. Another grabbed for his gun but Sam had already pulled his out. This man followed the first man and now only two were left. They slowly raised their hands now and showed they were not willing for more action.

At Sam's command, the two men slowly loosened their gun belts and dropped them to the floor. Joe meanwhile began searching the men for any hidden weapons. They were clean. Both men now were willing to talk to Sam. The leader of the group who was now dead had hired them. They had been paid $500 up front for their services. Sam was not really concerned about how they came here but that now they would not be killing anyone. He took the two back to a cell and put them there. They would be up for trial now also. One of the men told Sam that this was the Woodruf Gang that had been hired by some Mexican officials to get their men back. This had not worked out so things would be over soon.

Now Sam was ready for another drink, but did not want to leave the prisoners alone now. He managed to have a bottle in a desk drawer so he poured Joe and him a drink. Joe asked Sam if he wanted him to stand by here for the night. They could alter shifts awake in case anything else came up. Sam accepted this so they relaxed and made ready for the night. Joe had everything he needed here so the watch began. Sam went back to a bed to rest for a while and left Joe sitting awake as a guard. The night passed very quiet and things were good in the morning.

Sam walked to the Prosecutors at eight in the morning and advised him of the incident from last night. This was a new twist to things now and the prosecutor went to work. He would approach the Judge to see when they might be tried. Joe sat in the office for this and then both walked to the café for a late breakfast. Sam ordered meals for the prisoners also and a local lad usually delivered this. Court was due to start again at 10. Joe was expecting the new trial would begin this day. He sent a message back to headquarters and walked to the court.

CHAPTER SIXTEEN

The court ended the previous trial by the sentences. The Judge sentenced each man to be hung since there was murder involved with this case. This was a standard at this time. The Judge did not want to start the new case however so it was set for two days from now. Joe was concerned but Sam told him he probably would not be needed. He would ask the Judge later about this. Joe felt like he was almost a prisoner now also. Now Sam had some things to get started for the hangings. He told Joe to take a break and catch a nap since neither had much sleep from last night. Joe felt this was a good idea.

Sam coordinated the hanging agenda and Joe got some rest. He would manage for this day and would be ready for helping with the hangings. Headquarters sent another message and told Joe to hang here for now until he was free from everything. They figured this was more important than anything else right now. Evening came around and Joe walked to the Sheriff's office.

"So everything ready for the executions now?" Joe asked.

"Yes. Things should go fairly well. I am glad you will be here to help if needed." Sam replied.

"You think we might need to carry the same schedule here for tonight?" Joe asked.

"Can't see why now. Let's get a bottle and do some sipping here for a while. I really do need to be here just in case." Sam said.

"Great. Be right back." Joe said as he walked out the door.

The two lawmen sat in the office and passed the evening in peace. They retired when a deputy arrived to sit out the night in the office to watch over the prisoners. No problems came during the night and morning found everyone up and working toward the executions set for this day. The Judge had selected the time as 11 am. A second time had been set for 12 since there were more condemned men than the gallows could handle at one time. The normal crowd was there as the sentences were carried out. There were no problems and once both sets were finished then the lawmen had time to sit and rest. Such things were not enjoyed by most of them. It was only acceptable when the knowledge of their individual crimes was known. The only thing on hold now was the trial for the last two men that had burst into the Sheriff's office.

CHAPTER SEVENTEEN

Joe rolled over and squinted at the sun shining through the window in his room. It was time to get moving. He generally did not sleep in but the last few days had been hard on him. Today would be the trial for the two remaining prisoners the Sheriff had. Joe's headquarters had been waiting and Joe finally wired them that everything here was concluded regarding him. He was now free to handle whatever they had waiting. Joe's assignment was to head for Fort Bowie and wire when he arrived there. This was to be a secret assignment so Joe was asked not to tell anyone his destination for now. Joe spent the remaining day here and he would leave in the morning. His service would not be needed for the hanging of the two remaining men if they were sentenced to that.

Joe walked to the rail station and booked passage to Benson. He would travel there and then ride horseback on. This was just a precaution against anyone watching him. This was common practice by Arizona Rangers when they were on a tight-lipped assignment. He would also gather some trail rations from the store here. This would appear normal for a Ranger as they usually were on the trail by themselves. After Joe had completed all this he sat down on a bench and waited for Sam to be finished with the trial. They hopefully could have some peace for the rest of the day.

At 1 the court should be recessed for lunch. Joe figured Sam would be available for something and they both could get a bite from the saloon with their set-outs. Joe sat without paying much attention to the time or the street. A couple of shots rang out down the street and Joe jumped up to see what was going on. He could tell a deputy had cornered a man and another deputy was running toward the court building. Joe headed that way. He had no idea what had happened. He arrived at the scene of the incident and saw immediately what had happened. Sam was lying on the boardwalk just outside the courtroom door. Joe looked at Sam and could tell that Sam was no longer here. He had been shot through the throat and probably died instantly. The deputy had immediately grabbed the man that had shot and he had this man bleeding from his head where the deputy's pistol had met it. The other deputy was checking the area for other gunmen and also collecting witnesses. Joe was set back by Sam's death but he jumped right in to help the deputies as he could. He had not seen anything however so they would depend on the deputy that did see everything and what other witnesses they could gather.

Joe got a couple of men carry Sam to the undertakers when the deputy in charge agreed to this. Joe was useless for helping the deputy in charge now. He had seen nothing and could not testify to anything. He was actually sorry he had not gone to the court trial. Joe walked to the undertakers and intended to pay for a tribute headstone for this brave lawman. Sam had worked in law since he was a young man. He had served very honorably and provided citizens with the best he could give them.

CHAPTER SEVENTEEN

Joe next went to the telegraph office and sent a wire off to headquarters. He did not ask for more time here since he knew there was nothing he could do. Sam would not have appreciated a lawman that put his duty aside for a funeral. Joe knew he would miss his friend but things turned this way many times. He never knew when he might be on the receiving end of such an incident. Joe sat outside the telegraph office and was thinking of all that had happened lately. He was getting tired of being the man on the line and moving around a lot. He had always liked this about his Ranger job but because of the latest incidents he was having second thoughts. This was not unusual as it happened after days like this. He knew he would drive on and soon be back into his normal mood.

Joe walked to the hotel livery and checked on Jean. He always checked on her daily if possible. He talked with the young lad that was working there and the boy had some questions for Joe. He was trying to get a direction to go with a lifetime occupation. He had always been interested in the Rangers and was thinking about this. The Rangers only hired men after they were 25 years of age. They generally wanted men that were settled down after they had sowed some wild oats.

The time came for Joe to board the train for Benson. He loaded Jean into the baggage car and climbed aboard the passenger car. A few minutes later the train jolted and began slowly moving out from the station. Joe sat watching the town disappear. There were only a couple other people in this car. Both passengers appeared to be businessmen dressed in suits. Joe was staring out the window and had many mixed thoughts running through his mind. He was at the place now of needing to get away and be completely by himself. Such times were the salvation for Joe.

The train pulled into Benson about two hours later and Joe retrieved Jean and saddled up to ride off. He did stop by the Marshals office to see him and find out if there had been any trouble in this area.

"Hello George. Glad to see you are still doing nothing." Joe said as he entered the office.

"I'm so far behind I think I'm ahead. Heard about Sam and he was a good man." George stated.

"Yup. I was sitting along the street and he was about a block down the street. I didn't see a thing but one deputy did." Joe told George

"Makes a person wonder if they might end up like this." George stated.

George pulled a bottle from his desk drawer and poured them a drink. Things looked fairly peaceful around here so Joe sat back and sipped his drink.

"Heard anything from Tombstone?" Joe asked.

"Nope. Just peaceful I guess. The Marshal came through here after the trial in Tucson and stopped for a few minutes. He seemed to be pleased about the rapid court wrap up of things." George stated.

The two lawmen sat for a few minutes and then Joe needed to get moving. He bid George goodbye and rode off. He indicated to George he was heading toward Tombstone. This would keep any questions away for now. It was cool and the lone ride was a welcome thought to Joe. He now was thinking about Fort Bowie and what might be there for him. He usually did not spend much time around there since basically the army was the main residents. A few civilians were divided between ranching and small stores for service to others. Indian problems were not a concern anymore either.

Joe took three days to ride to Fort Bowie and he had enjoyed his time alone. Law enforcement at times could get very trying and he could only gain back his resolve by riding off alone. Joe rode up to the headquarters building at Fort Bowie and tied Jean up. He mounted the steps and a corporal greeted him at the door. Evidently this man knew why he was here, as things seem to be expecting him. The

CHAPTER SEVENTEEN

Commanding Officer, Major Smith was out of his office to meet Joe also.

"Nice to see you again Joe. How have things been?" The Major asked as he motioned for Joe to go to his office.

"Not too bad except for loosing Sam back in Tucson." Joe replied.

"Yeah, I heard about that. Too bad. That man was the real thing." The Major said.

"Well, what has been so bad around here that you needed me?" Joe asked.

"Well, we have something growing here that I really don't like. A few men moved into this area a couple of weeks ago." The Major said. "I think they might have come from Texas and probably were no good men there also.

"That happens at times." Joe agreed.

"Well things could get fairly sticky now. Seems these jerks want to dig up trouble with some Apache around here. They were involved with the nations back around Texas but since that has changed they ran out of things to do." The Major stated.

"Damn. Don't they know what they could trigger here?" Joe asked.

"I think they are hoping for something like that since they get their fun that way." The Major said. "And there is some rumor that a couple of these men had relatives involved with the Apache Pass thing years ago."

"Where are these men staying around here?" Joe asked.

"Not real sure but they seem to be camping out of the post." The Major said.

"Well I guess my first move is to find out where they are camping. After that I might be able to shut them down with some logical sense but you can never tell." Joe stated.

"Well I was hoping you could do something. The army is really tied regarding things until the situation gets out of hand." The Major said.

A WASTELAND OF OUTLAWS

The two men sat and talked for a few minutes then the Major invited Joe to dine with him. He had managed to hire a fairly good cook for him and his officers here. This was a great dividend for a lonely army post out in nowhere land. There were some things that a person could accomplish if they tried. Fort Bowie was heading to be closed by the army, since most trouble was no longer a concern. The west was changing rapidly now and things were coming close to a civilized lifestyle. Joe was not sure if this was going to be good or not.

Chapter Eighteen

As evening arrived, Joe took a stroll outside the fort. He was thinking about these men the commander had told him about. It seemed that when things looked real good for a peaceful future, something had to mess things up. Joe sat down on a log and watched the sunset. This was one of the most beautiful things in Arizona. The coming night seemed peaceful and Joe was hoping for a good couple of days so he could check around the area for these new people. He sat here for a few more minutes then walked back into the fort and headed toward the saloon. He would get a nightcap and head to the bed. Joe wanted to be up early and out riding the close area.

Joe entered the saloon and a man called to him. He looked at the table the man was sitting and saw it was Fred Jones, an old white scout for the army. Fred had been around for many years and knew more about this area than the Indians. Joe walked to the table.

"Hello you old horse thief." Joe spoke.

"Well that is a nice thing to call your old buddy." Fred said.

"Wasn't expecting to see you around here. Figured the Indians might have taken you out by now." Joe said. "Guess they are losing their touch also."

"Bet I can think why you're here." Fred said. "There is a feeling hanging around the area and I really don't care for it."

"Feeling?" Joe spoke looking straight at Fred. "I have learned you don't get feelings over nothing. What are you seeing Fred?"

"Well not much yet, but I see some movement around and things aren't appearing as they should. You talk with the commander yet?" Fred asked.

"Yeah. You seem to be in tune to things. Any chance this could get out of hand easy?" Joe asked.

"The next three days will tell you that. Can't see any delay if something is coming. Saw a lot of Indian hunters out and they were moving more like a war party than a hunting one." Fred said pointing to the south. "Most action is down that way and they are in their home territory.

"You feel like riding out in the morning with me for a time?" Joe asked. "I need to scope out some of the area."

"Sure. I think the commander can get along without me for a little while." Fred said.

The two men had another drink and then walked to their quarters. Tomorrow would be a start and Joe was hoping that things would stay peaceful until he had a chance to find out some good information. Joe undressed and rolled into his bedroll. His room had a rope spring bed and it felt fairly nice now. He didn't wait long before he was into dreamland.

Morning arrived and Joe was up greeting it. He walked to the mess hall and grabbed some fast breakfast. Fred found him there and he got a fast bite also. They would be out before long and Joe already had some trail rations

Chapter Eighteen

from his trip here. Fred always managed to keep some chow in his saddlebags in case of his need to go out. After they had eaten both walked to the stables and saddled up. They rode out of the post and headed in a southwesterly direction. Fred mentioned that he figured this area was a major pivot point for any trouble that might be coming. The air was just a little bit sharp this early but the sun would soon warm this. As the men rode along both were watching carefully around them. They did not need to talk as they rode basically since both knew what the other was doing. They had worked together in the past.

By midmorning they were seeing various signs of braves around the area. There was something different out here and things were giving the appearance of a different day. This was an alarm for the two men and they were getting very careful with their observations. The signs from the Indians did not indicate they were concerned about anything but there was still a feeling the two men had that things were not normal. Joe had the feeling that the hair on his neck was standing straight up. Fred mentioned that his seemed to be doing that also. Finally both men stopped and looked around very carefully. They dismounted without anything being said and moved carefully over to some rocks. Here they settled down for a time to watch the area.

"Sure can't figure all this out. I really haven't seen anything that gives an appearance of danger or other things in this area." Fred mentioned.

"Yup, I just can't clear this feeling however. Guess I've been in the bush too much lately." Joe said.

The two sat quietly for over a half hour. Both were constantly watching around them. Finally they both saw some men at the same time. These appeared to be white men riding to the south. There were six men and they didn't seem to be concerned about anyone else seeing them. They rode into sight of Joe and Fred about 500 yards off. They were riding on and Fred scanned the far horizon. Now he saw some heavy trouble ahead of the six men. There was a small band of Indian braves on the top of a small crest in the landscape. These men appeared to be watching the six men also. Half of the braves suddenly disappeared to the rear of the group and Fred knew this was an indication they were prepared for battle.

"Looks like things could heat up shortly." Fred said quietly

"Sure does." Joe answered.

The six men were getting close to the last location that the braves had been seen. Three braves now were seen riding toward the six on the level with them. The two groups came together and it appeared they were talking. Then a puff of smoke was seen from the six men. As a brave fell from his horse, the sound of the gunshot reached Joe's ears. Now the six men were riding hard back the direction they had come from. At the same time, the rest of the band of the braves came charging toward the six white men. A running gunfight was in progress now as the white men raced back the direction they came from. As Joe and Fred watched this scene, the sight of white puffs of smoke was seen from a hillside to the right of the six men. Two of these men slumped in their saddles as they raced on. The Indians evidently had carefully considered the possibility of action like this. A few seconds later another white man slumped in his saddle then fell to the ground. Now for some reason the braves quit the chase.

The five men still on their mounts sped on and did not stop to see about their wounded comrade. The Indians moved off and now Fred and Joe mounted up to see about the man on the ground. They rode up and checked the man. He was hit hard but still alive. Joe was tending to the man and Fred rode off to get his horse. The horse had stopped about 500 feet from the man. The two men managed to get the wounded man on his horse and they headed back to the fort. Joe did not think the man would make the trip.

Chapter Eighteen

The two men set a good pace and arrived at the fort just after noon. They carried the wounded man to the hospital but there they found the man had died. A horse that was tied up in front of the headquarters appeared to be one like a man had been riding with the six earlier. Fred and Joe walked inside. They could hear the man talking in a loud voice with the commander. His story from what they heard was much different from the actual happening. Joe walked to the door of the commander's office and paused. The commander invited them inside and they sat listening to the story the man was telling. According to him the six had been riding out looking for stray cattle and the Indians rode up to them and started shooting for no reason. One of the men was dead and the other two badly wounded. The story was interesting to Joe and Fred but they kept quiet until the man had finished.

"I demand you do something about those murdering savages Major." The man raged.

"Don't know the whole story yet. Just hold your step for a minute." The Major replied. He turned toward Joe and Fred. "You two know anything about this?"

"Well sorta Major, but it ain't like this man is saying." Fred started. "We watched the entire incident from a high point."

"Yup, and these six men had a meeting with three braves. They shot one of the braves and rode off fast. They probably figured the three were alone." Joe stated.

"That's a damn lie Major. These two were nowhere around when this happened." The man said.

"Well I've known these two men for many years and they haven't told me a story yet." The Major stated. "I would take their story over yours anytime."

"These Indians around here are basically peaceful until they are pushed the wrong direction." Fred stated.

"Well we shall find out before long what happened." The Major said as he called for the corporal.

"Corporal, take this man to the post stockade and hold him for now." The Major said.

"You can't do that to me. I'm a citizen and you have to protect me!" The man shouted as the corporal led him off.

"We'll wait for a couple of days and see how things are off the post. If nothing shows yet then we need to contact some of these Apache and see what happened. I know it is like you two said but I need to know if they have any other thoughts." The Major said.

"Well we should know probably by the end of the day." Fred said.

"Let's hope things are not too cranked up over this. If needed I think Fred and I can make contact and talk with the braves." Joe said.

"Well, we shall wait and see. Meanwhile you two get some R&R." The Major said.

Joe and Fred left the headquarters and walked to the post saloon. Things were feeling fairly good now and they hoped the braves would not fly off the handle before seeing what else might be around. A few men were sitting in the saloon and the two men heard as soon as they entered that the conversation had been about the day's activities. Two men were telling stories and Joe figured they were with the other man in the incident. When Joe and Fred walked in the place turned an icy reception for them. The bartender served them and he looked at Joe and raised his eyes and moved his head toward the two men. Joe knew what he was saying. These men would not be able to gather much backing from anyone around here. The place had been at peace and not much chance of any problems unless the braves were pushed into it.

"Hey Fred. These guys are saying you are not much for telling the truth about injuns. They seem to think you and Joe are just amateurs in dealing with them." Jake, a friend said.

This did not set well with the three men but they kept their cool for now. Fred was almost hoping they might start

Chapter Eighteen

something. Everyone in the post knew Fred and his long held abilities in knowing Indians. Shortly the two men left the saloon, which ended problems for now.

CHAPTER NINETEEN

Joe and Fred sat for a time in the saloon and then they walked outside. The fort was quiet and the evening air was refreshing. The two men sat watching the soldiers wondering around the post and felt things were very peaceful here. Both secretly hoped things stayed like this. They would see how things were in the morning. Joe wanted to attempt a journey into the native land area to talk with some natives. This would tell more than anything what might be going. Joe figured that he and Fred could meet with the chiefs of the area and not be held in any trouble.

"We might see if we can borrow Grayhorse from the Major tomorrow." Joe stated. Grayhorse was an Indian scout and was very strong with his people also.

"We need to see if Grayhorse will ride out and set a meeting up for us. That would be much easier and probably safer if the natives are a little bit in an uproar." Fred agreed.

The two men now walked to the mess hall and got some supper. One nice thing about Fort Bowie was they feed almost anyone that came around. This was basically a treat for anyone riding in. Travel rations were not much when a person was riding around the wilds. The men that had been in the saloon earlier were not at the mess hall. Joe wondered if they were still at the fort or had ridden off. The Major had mentioned the men in question were camping somewhere out from the fort.

The men ate and then walked back outside. Both stood for a minute on the porch of the mess building and looked things over around the post. Things were normal so they walked to the saloon and took a table. They would relax here a few minutes and then hit the sack. The saloon was not very well attended this night. The soldiers must either be busy or out of money. The owner here would run a tab for the soldiers but the Major was not pleased when his men ran up a large account.

The two men finally went to their quarters and got needed rest for the coming day. Things were hopefully going to look better then. Joe would see about getting Grayhorse and then they could ride off toward the distance native areas where the Chiefs generally stayed. The night ran peacefully by and soon it was daylight again.

The two met outside the barracks and headed for the mess hall. There they met with the Major who was getting a bite also.

"Major, we would like to borrow Grayhorse for a couple of days. We need to get a meeting with the natives if possible and find out what might be needed to stem a new uprising around here." Joe stated.

"That is no problem with me. You need to check with him however. I never allow a scout to be used without their agreement." The Major replied.

"Great, then we will see and if things are ok we will ride off shortly. Hope we can guide any problems away." Joe stated.

Grayhorse was found and Joe with Fred talked with him. He was happy to assist them. He did mention that he hoped the Chiefs would not be in a bad mood. He would be on the line if such were found. Joe walked to the headquarters and advised the Major of the situation and they would be riding off. Fred and Grayhorse got their steeds ready and Fred was saddling Jean when Joe returned. The three men mounted up and rode out of the post.

The morning was crisp but it felt good to the men as they rode. As they rode the three talked about the upcoming meeting. Grayhorse felt the Chiefs would be happy to meet with Joe and Fred. They had always thought a lot regarding these men. Grayhorse was among them as far as appreciating the work of Joe and Fred. The three were not riding hard since they needed to keep the horses fresh for the long ride that might lie ahead.

The three men had been riding for about two hours when suddenly a shot rang out to the side. The lead missed them but they were instantly dismounted and grabbing some shelter. Now other shots were sounding from a small hill to the east of them. Grayhorse was glued to the hill and soon saw the opposition. At first he saw what appeared to be natives. He stared hard at the men and then noticed a difference. These men were not wearing normal dress of the local natives.

"Those are not my people." Grayhorse stated. "They dress like us but have wrong gear and headdress."

"Ok, guess that is one thing in our favor. We need to work toward them and maybe we can get one to find out just who they really are." Fred said.

The three started moving around as they could, keeping out of a clear shot by the others. They also were shooting toward the hill as they moved. Slowly they managed to work closer to the hill and the other side was maintaining their fire toward the three. Things were beginning to appear as if it would be rather warm here shortly. At this point Joe had counted at least six men firing at them. Over a half hour the three had worked toward the hill about 300 yards. The other side was giving no indication they were going to leave.

Then Joe recognized a sound coming from the north. It was a bugle sounding a charge for the cavalry. Before long the soldiers rode hard up to the area. The fight was now strongly sided with the three men. Within ten minutes, the soldiers had captured or killed all the opposing side. They had seven live men at this point. They were dressed poorly as natives and even the soldier could tell they were really white men. This evidently had been a trap to catch the three men and make it appear as if the natives had been the attackers.

Lieutenant Sacks had led the charging group of soldiers. He told Joe that the Major had formed this force shortly after the three had left the fort. He was afraid they might have some problems. The rescue force had arrived in time and now they had prisoners to hold. This was a federal crime now since the attack was made on Army Scouts. Lieutenant Sacks and the three men sat down for a few minutes and discussed this attack and what might be in the future for the three. Grayhorse spoke up and advised that the natives would not be involved in such activity. He also indicated that the natives close by probably had seen the fight. If the cavalry had not arrived when it did, the natives probably would have stepped in and finished things.

The Lieutenant called for his men and they mounted up to return to the fort. Joe and Fred thanked them for their rescue. The three men mounted up also and headed south. Grayhorse had already planned a stop for the evening. He was thinking that this might be a place to wait while he ventured on to talk with the Chiefs. His chosen spot had good water and grass besides some game for evening meat. There was a good feeling among the three now and they looked forward to a good venture as they moved on.

The trail was good and there was no other threats seen by the men as they moved forward. On occasion Grayhorse would indicate that certain natives were observing their movement and he was sure they knew who the three were. The natives knew all three men and all were accepted as good, strong men that strove for peace above all else. The three men did not cast their vigilance aside however since there might be more white men around that did not want them messing with plans they might have set into motion.

The three rode along until about 4 in the afternoon. They arrived at the campsite Grayhorse had selected for them. They soon were set down for a few hours and Fred had built a small fire for warming some beans over. Grayhorse slipped out of camp and returned in a few minutes with two rabbits for meat. The site was rather nice now and the small fire would be seen by other natives and appreciated since they never understood why white men needed huge fires in a campsite.

After they had eaten Joe produced a bottle. They sat around and sipped on the drink. Grayhorse had gained the habit from the white men but also knew his limit. He was very cautious when drinking since he had seen white men get goofy and killed by stupid actions while they were influenced by alcohol. There was little talking now among the three. They were relaxing and all thinking of tomorrow. What might come from all this could be a glorious peace or a full frontier war. It seemed odd that the hopes of both sides really sat here in this camp.

Finally the men rolled up in their sleeping gear and eased off to sleep. The night passed quietly and when the morning sun greeted the land the three were up and ready for this new day. Grayhorse would move out and hopefully gain a meeting with the natives before long. The main stronghold that Cochise had used for years was only a few miles away. It was still used by the main Chiefs and it was a safe sanctuary from others that might wish to fight these natives. Joe and Fred arranged themselves in the camp for a stay of unknown length. They could do nothing until Grayhorse returned.

"Any bets how long it might take Grayhorse?" Joe asked.

"Couldn't get even close. At least we know that we are known to the local natives and basically thought as fairly good guys." Fred responded.

Time seemed to pass with the speed of a snail. There really wasn't much the two men could do but stand by. The hours passed and the two men sat looking at each other and the various noises about them. They could hear squirrels and birds around and this did give them some entertainment. About two in the afternoon they were jarred back into alert status by a man walking toward the camp. It was a native. The brave walked proudly up to the camp and handed Joe a large piece of meat. Joe thanked him and he nodded and left. It was sure now that the local Indians knew they were here. It was not telling them how long Grayhorse might be gone however. The meat was given them for food while they waited. This was a very good sign at any rate. The day grew on and finally the men ate some of the meat and lay on their bedrolls. No sign or word from Grayhorse.

The night passed with both men sleeping lightly and waking at the slightest noise. Morning found no Grayhorse yet and so the two men started out on a second day in the camp. They could really do nothing until they heard from Grayhorse or he returned. This day would be slower than the last since both men were anxious to get things going. The morning passed slowly and still no sign from Grayhorse. Joe was getting a little anxious but Fred told him Grayhorse would be fine and they just had to wait for him.

CHAPTER TWENTY

The day passed and about 4 both men were getting a little edgy. Fred had figured that things should have been arranged by noon. No Grayhorse or any word about him. Joe scratched around the old fire ring and set a new fire for supper. It would provide heat for some meat and that was about all either man was interested in eating right now. Supper was cooked and they ate. Now it was time to just sit and wait again. It was just getting to dusk and both men heard a noise outside the camp. They immediately were on the alert, watching carefully toward the invading dark. Two men walked close and hailed the camp. Fred answered and invited them in.

The men appeared to be cowhands but there was no known ranch in this area. The men sat down and accepted a cup of coffee.

"What the Hell are you guys camping clear out here for?" One man asked.

"Seemed to give a decent place for a camp. We just stopped here and will move on toward Tombstone in the morning." Fred replied.

"Did you have any idea that this is Indian Territory?" The other man asked.

"Hell most everywhere is right now. We didn't expect to be bothered by them however since we are showing no attempt to hide." Joe mentioned.

"That is probably easy for you to say if you don't know about these local Indians. They have been known to attack even other natives in their area." One man stated.

"Well I've have been around here for a time and never seen much that might indicate hostile actions." Fred said.

"What are you two doing out here?" Joe asked.

"We are heading a little north. We were working on a ranch down by Bisbee and the boss was taken by some lawmen and hung in Tucson. We need work now." One man stated.

"Well you can stay here for the night if you wish. We are all set down and the local natives know we are here." Fred said.

"How the Hell do they know you're here?" A man asked.

"We are known to the locals here. I work for the Army out of Fort Bowie." Fred said.

"Damn! How did we manage to stumble into this camp?" One man asked the other.

"You both might as well stay here for the night. We have some meat for your supper." Joe said.

"Well we could use something to eat. Been a ways on the trail so far and not much for small game." One of the men stated.

"Well, you might enjoy this meat since it was given by some natives yesterday. We are waiting to see some of them again." Fred stated.

"What the Hell do you want to see them about?" one of the men asked.

"Hope to get some peaceful talk in to help settle this area more. Men like you too often travel through here and cause problems you don't even understand." Joe stated.

"Well I'll be damned! We found ourselves a couple of Injun lovers Jake!" One man stated.

"Just understand what we said and you will be fine. Any attempts to change things will surely put you into the express for the Pearly Gates!" Joe spoke.

"Sure mister. Didn't mean anything by the remark Dan made." Jake stated. "We would like to stay for the night if that offer is still open."

"Yup. You also now know the rules." Fred stated.

Joe stirred the fire and got a flame going. He started cooking some of the meat. The two cowboys sat and watched Joe as he worked. Fred had moved back from the area a way and was watching the valley below as the sun began falling in the West. Fred looked to the small rises across the small valley and he could see some eyes there. He knew who it was and really was fairly pleased.

Joe watched him and when he returned to the fire he asked, "See anything there?"

"Yup. There are eyes there and they definitely know all that are here now." Fred stated.

"What you mean?" Jake asked

"Just some scouting eyes. They are probably wondering what you two are doing here." Joe stated. "Sure hope you haven't done anything against the natives lately."

"Not us thank God." Dan said.

I didn't think we were that close to natives." Jake said.

"Well now you know." Joe stated.

About this time, Grayhorse slid into the camp silently. Joe and Fred had seen him coming but the other two had no idea.

"You guys found some loose cowboys I see." Grayhorse stated. "Good thing they came here. The natives are not really happy with most white men right now."

"Mainly over the thing the other day with the six whites?" Joe asked.

"Well that also. But there have been some other things that we never knew about. Seems a lot of cattle have disappeared from the natives. They also have problems with small groups out hunting." Grayhorse stated.

"Seems every time we get things about fixed, some stupid white man has to mess it up!" Fred stated.

"These two men have to leave in the morning. They have been seen and will have safe conduct to Fort Bowie. Guess they haven't caused any trouble around here." Grayhorse stated.

"We sure as Hell will be gone. Don't like all this." Jake stated.

Everyone managed to get some food and Grayhorse had not eaten either. The talk around the campfire was general now. Grayhorse was not saying much about his meeting and it appeared he wouldn't until the other two left. Fred cleaned up the fire area and the others took care of the horses. The two other men were advised to unsaddle their mounts, as it would look funny to the natives if they didn't. The natives were not trusting most white men.

Joe brought out the bottle after everyone was finished with the normal night chores. The two white men looked funny when Grayhorse took a turn with the bottle. Neither said anything however. Finally everyone was ready for bed. Fred made sure that the two other white men knew not to wonder off during the night. This would not be acceptable to the natives who probably were watching the camp.

Morning arrived and a bright clear sky was beautiful. As everyone started getting things going for the day, Grayhorse stirred the fire and started breakfast. The two white men watched and didn't say anything. Everyone ate beans and meat with some hardtack for breakfast. During the meal, Joe advised the two men they needed to get on the trail immediately after eating. The natives would be watching and expect this.

When the time arrived, the men mounted their horses and Fred made sure they knew which way to head to stay healthy. As the rode off, Grayhorse gave the other two the information. The native Chiefs had not been overly happy to see Grayhorse. They were upset still about the small band of men that were stirring things up. Grayhorse had finally managed to get an audience from them for Joe and Fred.

The meeting was set for noon so as fast as everyone could get ready they moved out. The Chiefs had selected a site for the meeting and Grayhorse was strongly told not to bring the other two men in the camp. Joe had figured this already. The meeting place was about 15 miles so they should get there in plenty of time.

A WASTELAND OF OUTLAWS

CHAPTER TWENTY-ONE

A s soon as the other two men were gone Grayhorse advised they should get moving also. It was time to get on with the duties and hope that an arrangement might be obtained for the future of both races in this area. The three men cleaned up the camp and set off following Grayhorse. Joe maintained a watch back toward the camp in case the other two men might decide to follow. The ride was slow and the morning was very nice. Joe loved days like this. It was what had originally sold him on Arizona.

The trail was easy and the three closed in on the meeting place about 11:30. Grayhorse asked the others to hang a little back until the correct time was near. He would go ahead and see what might be in the wind at this time.

"Guess we must be about there so things should be turning around shortly." Joe stated.

"Things will go better with me once this is all finished." Fred stated.

Grayhorse now became visible ahead of the two. He motioned for them to come where he was. It appeared this might be the beginning for the meeting. Fred and Joe rode up and then dismounted when they came up to Grayhorse. This was an honorable gesture for the natives. Grayhorse took the three horses and tied them up to small brush plants close by. He led Fred and Joe to a large flat stone on the ground. This would be the meeting place. The Chiefs would be arriving very soon. The white men were not to sit until all parties were here.

At the right time horses were heard coming. The Chiefs rode up close and dismounted. Each gave the white men a signal of salute and they gathered around the large stone. The main Chief signaled to the white men to sit and everyone sat down around the rock. Grayhorse was requested as an interpreter even though two of the Chiefs spoke good English.

As usual the affair started off very slow. Much standard protocol was used in efforts to get everyone used to the others. Joe knew about most of this and the Chiefs all knew both men well. Minutes passed and finally the head Chief began conversation regarding recent activity in the area. Much talk around the subject was presented and no solution given. The talks continued for three hours. The Chiefs then called a truce with the talks for food. All personnel at the conference were feed and a relaxing calm was felt.

Talk began again after everyone had eaten. The procedure for all this was as the Chiefs wished. Joe was beginning to see a focus in the near future. As evening came slowly upon the group, a halt was called for the talks for the day. Everyone would spend the night here and continue in the morning. Joe and Fred were fed well and they made their beds up for the night. Joe would have appreciated a drink but this would not be welcome here.

"Surely hope tomorrow is the end with a good agreement." Fred stated.

"Yes. I think it might come around to that early tomorrow." Joe said. "This day has about to get the best of me. I think I will sleep good tonight."

The pressure of the meeting probably had strained all those in attendance. The Chiefs had even looked a bit tired. Every one was soon asleep as the darkness moved in. Joe and Fred slept sound and awoke with the daylight. The natives here were already up. Beds were picked up and after some morning food, the talks started.

This day the talks headed straight into the current problems here. The Chiefs were concerned about their existence if fights began close by. They would not start anything but there was no promise about white men moving in the area. Joe knew about this and he could only state that the white men in charge would not accept fighting people in this area. They would require the white men in the area to give wide birth to any Indian people seen. The white man words would not be accepted without complete investigation.

Around noon, the talks had tapered down and the end was seen very close. Joe and Fred knew not to ask for a signed paper from the natives. They did not trust paper documents. An Indian would give his word and this was more solid than any paper. Joe told the Chiefs not to place themselves or their men in danger when encountering white men. If danger were present then action would have to be taken for the safety of everyone.

The Chiefs accepted the results of this talk and they were pleased that Joe and Fred were the ones involved from the white man's group. Goodbyes were given and everyone packed up their personal things and set off in the direction they had come from. Joe and Fred were pleased with the outcome of these talks. They planned to ride until nightfall and camp where they might get water. The fort was still a strong days ride after this day. They needed to get back to give the military the information they had.

The night was peaceful and the three men moved out the next morning. Grayhorse rode ahead to scout in case anything might be planned ahead of them. Just before noon Grayhorse observed some men on horseback. They appeared to be natives but they were not riding as natives. He stopped and watched these men. He was far enough from the group that they probably wouldn't see him. They seemed to be moving in a deliberate way toward a section that had large rocks. Grayhorse soon figured these men were not up to good. He rode back and advised Joe and Fred of the situation ahead.

The three men sat for a short time discussing the situation. They finally decided to press ahead and see what developed. Joe had noticed that the three were being watched. He saw evidence of this and these were not white men. The three moved for about an hour and they came close to the rock section. Grayhorse advised the other two of this and everyone was on full alert. When the three were about 400 yards from the rocks, rifle fire sudden filled the air. Fred was nicked in the right leg. The three rode hard back from the area. Once they reached a place far enough from the rocks they set down. Joe was watching the men as he could see them. They were dressed as Indians but he noticed as Grayhorse had, they were riding horses with full saddle equipment. Natives seldom rode like this.

The three men worked their way ahead toward the rocks and made sure they had some cover for protection. They ended up about 150 yards from the rocks and shots were ringing out steady. Joe noticed that they were creating some problems for the group with loss of four or five men. The battle continued and things were heating up. Joe now heard a familiar noise. A bugle was sounding to the north. The cavalry came charging in and soon had everything under control.

CHAPTER TWENTY-ONE

The commander at the fort had ordered Lt Rems out. He was concerned about this sort of problem. The soldiers took six men into custody and the rest were beyond help. The fort would send a team out to bury them later.

The three moved on at a faster pace now. They were all anxious to get to the post this night. The landmarks were becoming better known now and Joe guessed they were about five miles from the post. As the three topped the last hill from the post they observed a stage running east below them. It was probably heading toward Lordsburg. The post offered the stage a stop for the night hours. This was part of the Butterfield Stage Line yet.

About an hour later, the three rode into the post and each had a sigh of relief to be back. Fred and Joe headed to the headquarters to see the Major and Grayhorse rode toward the corral to get his horse bedded down. The Major was still in his office and he heard the two men come in. He jumped up and almost ran out to the main room to see them.

"Sure good to see you guys." The Major stated. "You have any luck with the Chiefs?"

"We think so. Lets go into your office and we will tell you all about it." Fred told him.

They all walked into the office and Joe closed the door. He wasn't sure but felt this stuff should be held in confidence for now. The Major grabbed a bottle from his desk and set out three glasses. He poured each a good drink and sat down at his desk. Joe and Fred began to tell the story.

Grayhorse was unsaddling his horse when another man walked into the corral area. He walked toward Grayhorse and shoved him.

"Get outa my way injun." The man said gruffly.

Grayhorse caught himself before he fell over. He did not say anything. The white man noticed all this and came close to him.

"You got nothing to say injun?" The man said. He then took a swing at Grayhorse. The man didn't see if his swing hit Grayhorse or not. A soldier had arrived and dropped the man with an axe handle.

"Sorry about that Grayhorse. Seems this jerk doesn't have much for manners." The soldier stated.

Grayhorse smiled at the soldier. "Thanks. I didn't want to provoke the man."

"Well, I'll advise my sergeant and the incident will get out. This is one of the men the Major has been holding here until you guys made it back." The soldier told Grayhorse.

The soldier walked to the door of the stables and called out. "Sergeant of the Guard. Stables."

The sergeant came on a run and arrived to see the other man still lying on the ground. The soldier advised the sergeant what had happened. The sergeant told the soldier to get another man and drag this one to the guardhouse.

"You ok Grayhorse?" the sergeant asked.

"Yes. I managed to duck his swing and he didn't have time for trying another, thanks to your soldier." Grayhorse told him.

"Well hope no one else bothers you Grayhorse. Let me know if you have any trouble." The sergeant said as he walked away.

"Thanks again Sergeant." Grayhorse said.

Grayhorse walked to his room where the other scouts stayed. They had their own food kitchen since many did not like much of the white food at the mess hall. Brown Beaver was cooking himself some supper.

"Smells good. Got any extra?" Grayhorse asked.

"Only for you. Grab your pan." Brown Beaver told him.

Now Joe and Fred had finished their initial report to the Major and they were heading to the mess hall.

"Should be good to get some real food now. Can't stand my own cookin let alone yours or Grayhorse's." Joe said.

CHAPTER TWENTY-ONE

They entered the mess hall and found the chow line. There was roast beef and potatoes tonight. Smelled almost like apple pie also. Fred and Joe proceeded to dig into their meal. A runner from the telegraph office came in, found Joe and handed him a wire. It was from headquarters. They requested Joe to hang around the post for a few days to make sure things would straighten out. The message was about a day old. Joe had not sent his report back to them yet. He figured there would be time in the morning. He and Fred were tired from their mission and only wanted food some drink and then bed.

After they had finished their supper, both men walked toward the saloon. As they approached, the door suddenly flew open and two men came sailing out. There was a fight in progress and this they did not need. Both stood outside for a few minutes. Soon a squad of soldiers came on the run. They entered the saloon and began hauling men out. There were three additional civilians plus a couple of soldiers. Soldiers seldom fought here as they faced severe punishment for that. The soldiers were hauled to the guardhouse for the night and the civilians were advised to leave the area for the night.

Joe recognized two of the civilians and they had been involved in the native problem he and Fred had witnessed last week. Joe wanted to talk with the soldiers involved but Fred told him to wait until morning. So they entered the saloon and sat down at a table.

The bartender brought them a bottle and glasses. They leaned back and sipped their drinks as they over the fight incident.

"Wonder what really was going on with things that set the soldiers off." Fred stated.

"Don't know but I'd bet it might be something about the natives and these jerky civilians." Joe stated.

"Was thinking the same thing. I hope we can find out more tomorrow. Things could go down hard if this continues." Fred said.

"We should find out more tomorrow." Joe said.

Both men sat and drank for a few minutes then decided to get some sleep. A person really never slept well when they were out on a mission like they had been.

CHAPTER TWENTY-TWO

Morning arrived and Joe had been up for almost an hour. He had been sitting in his room and thinking over the situation from last night. He had some concerns about these civilians and needed to see what the Major might think. Fred knocked on his door and Joe answered. They headed for the mess hall for some breakfast.

"So did you sleep good last night?" Fred asked.

"Like a log. Now I need to get breakfast and then seek out the two soldiers from last night." Joe said.

"We better see the Major first. He can provide bodies if he agrees with us." Fred stated.

Both men entered the mess hall and ate breakfast. After they had finished, they walked to the headquarters building. The corporal there advised the Major would be here in a few minutes. So both men sat down to wait. The corporal figured what they wanted.

"I imagine you are interested in the fight last night. That is what the Major is doing right now." The corporal stated.

"Any chance we can meet him over at the guardhouse?" Joe asked.

"Best just stay here. He doesn't like others involved with his military in things like this. He will talk to you as soon as he returns." The corporal stated.

As the time crept by the corporal would walk to the door and check out the area. Soon he advised that the Major was coming. Joe and Fred were anxious as the Major walked into the building.

"Hello you two. I imagine I know why you're here. Come into my office." The Major said.

Both men followed the Major into his office and Fred closed the door. Everyone was silent for a moment. Then the Major spoke.

"The situation last night could be nasty. I have hopefully stopped everything for now. Those men were all part of that last group in the confrontation with the natives before you guys left." The Major told them. "I have ordered these men held for trial here. That is about all I can do for now."

"I could arrest them also and have them arraigned for trial in Tucson if you wish." Joe stated.

"I was hoping you might say that. My authority is rather slim on civilians. I can only charge them with obstruction of an Army program." The Major stated.

"Well, we can handle this. Any chance you can give me an escort to Benson to catch the train to Tucson?" Joe asked.

"Done." The Major replied.

"Ok, lets get things going as soon as I see if headquarters has anything more important for me. They better not since I think this is the top." Joe stated.

"You can advise that I think these men will continue stirring the pot with the natives unless something is done to stop them." The Major added.

"Well I'll let you know as soon as I find out." Joe said as he walked out the door.

Joe walked to the telegraph office and sent a wire to headquarters. He asked the corporal there to send a runner as soon as he got a reply. He advised he would be over at the stables or the blacksmiths. Fred caught up with Joe now and they walked toward the stables.

"The Major is really heated up over all this. He hopes you can end these problems now." Fred stated.

"Yeh, I hope so too. I intend to charge those men with second degree murder which should hold them for a few years in Yuma." Joe stated.

The two men walked into the stables and Joe checked Jean over. She was appreciating her short rest. Her shoes were all good yet so Joe knew she was ready to go when he was. Fred also checked his mount and then they walked over to the corral. There were some nice broncos there the Army was going to try out. Joe always appreciated good horseflesh and these looked great. The two men stood there watching the horses and discussing things about them. A runner came from the telegraph and handed Joe a message. Headquarters had agreed for him to transport the prisoners to Tucson. They had nothing else for him now.

"Looks like I'll be headed for Tucson, maybe tomorrow." Joe stated.

"Better you than me." Fred answered. "I never did like that town."

"I really don't either but that's my duty." Joe stated.

They both headed back toward the headquarters now. The day was nice and warm and Joe hoped for a good day tomorrow. They arrived at the headquarters and walked in. The Major was there and he had seen them coming.

"You must have good news." The Major said.

"Well, I guess I'll transport the prisoners to Tucson. Hope you can still give me a squad to Benson." Joe stated. I intend to charge them with second-degree murder of the natives. That should hold them a while in Yuma."

"Great. You want to leave in the morning?" The Major asked.

"Yup." Joe stated.

"Ok, I'll arrange things." The Major stated.

Fred and Joe left the headquarters with the promise that the Major would advise when he had everything arranged. It was early but the two walked to the saloon. The man there put out some lunch items about noon and Joe thought that would be as good as the mess hall now. They entered the saloon and found only one other man there besides the bartender.

"Howdy men. What will it be today?" The bartender asked.

"Give us a couple of beers. We'll slip into things slowly for now." Fred smiled.

Fred and Joe stood at the bar now while the bartender fetched some lunch items. He had a good spread as Joe could see. This was going to be a good day after all. Both men started on the lunch items immediately. Both usually had good appetites when off the trail.

"Not very busy today?" Joe asked the bartender.

"Nope. Since the fight the other night, things have been down. The Major don't like such things in his post." The bartender stated.

"What did you think about the fight?" Joe asked.

"Well, seems like those yahoos were really against injuns and army." The bartender started. "They just kept laying things on the two soldiers here. The soldiers did real well until the men walked up close and grabbed at them. Then things kinda lit up."

"This is a lot more than we have heard from anyone else." Joe said.

"Well, I just wanted you two to know that things are not always the army's fault." The bartender spoke.

The two men had eaten their lunch now and ordered another beer. They stood around the saloon for another hour and discussed very little. Joe next decided to catch a nap for the afternoon and agree to meet Fred for supper at the mess hall.

It was after five when Joe rose up and walked toward the mess hall. He entered the building and planned on getting a cup of coffee if Fred wasn't there yet. He saw that he was almost late as Fred and the Major were already sitting at a table. He walked up and greeted them.

"I'll get some chow and come back." Joe told them. He walked to the chow line and got some food. Tonight was an Army special – Beans! They did have fresh biscuits anyway. He returned to the table and sat down.

"Guess you two have already solved the problems of the Territory. You can at least fill me in now." Joe stated.

"You'll have your squad at seven in the morning if you are ready to go." The Major stated.

"Any objection if I line them up my way?" Joe asked.

"If you mean with your ropes, I don't really care." The Major stated. "Your system is almost a legend around anymore."

"I'll finish here and then stop by the saloon. Need to get to bed early so I am fresh for the trail tomorrow." Joe stated.

A WASTELAND OF OUTLAWS

CHAPTER TWENTY-THREE

Morning arrived and Joe had been up for almost an hour. He had been sitting in his room and thinking over the situation coming up. He decided to get a breakfast, as stopping for lunch on the trail might not be an option. He walked to the mess hall and found Fred there also.

"Good morning." Joe greeted him.

"Morning. See you are up and ready." Fred replied. "I think I'll ride along with you this day. Might be nice for a short trip out."

The two ate their breakfasts and then headed to the stables. Jean was waiting and looked like she was ready to go. Joe saddled her and Fred got his horse ready. They walked them over to the headquarters. The Major met them outside and pointed to the squad that was getting ready to go.

"There are your men. They will only take you to Benson, then you are on your own." He told Joe.

"Good enough. I appreciate the assistance." Joe replied.

"I'm going along with the squad Major." Fred stated. "Thought it might be good to scout a little after recent things."

"Good. You come back with the squad though. Don't want you out there by yourself right now." The Major stated.

Joe and Fred mounted up and walked to the squad. They mounted as they seen the two coming.

"Howdy Joe. I'm in charge of this squad and we will take you to Benson." The Corporal stated.

The group headed out the gate and onto the road. The day was sunny already and Joe could feel the warmth creep into his bones. It was going to be a nice day. He hoped to make it to Benson in three days. If things went well they could. The squad had lined up the prisoners and they had put the noose rope on them for Joe. The squad had six men counting the Corporal. Joe and Fred rode behind the Corporal and three men were behind the prisoners. It all looked like a larger military patrol. Joe hoped the natives would see this. He knew they would appreciate the prisoners being taken west.

"Sure gonna be nice when they finish the railroad from Benson to Lordsburg." Fred stated.

"Yup. Save a lot of time in these trips. Probably won't need me much after that." Joe stated.

"Well Hell, you aren't much good now!" Fred laughed.

Joe began seeing eyes on high spots now. He smiled to himself and thought this was really good. Fred noticed all this too and he just nodded to Joe. The road did not have any traffic through this area. Joe was wondering how some people might take this group if they crossed paths. Many whites were still anti-native and there was always a chance of problems out on the trail. Joe was glad to have the Army with him. This would stop most things before anything was started.

CHAPTER TWENTY-THREE

The day ran well and about four Fred decided to ride ahead and see about a campsite for the night. Joe rode off with him and they figured the men could get another five miles yet. Joe knew of a good spot for a camp but it was almost eight miles ahead. The two covered about five miles and found nothing worth a stop.

"You think we can get three more miles before night?" Joe asked Fred.

"Guess we'd better from the looks of things right here. It will be nice to have water for the horses and us."

"Good. Come on and I can show you my spot." Joe replied.

They rode on and before long they arrived at Joe's spot. It was sheltered from the road enough and had water and grass around. There was some dried mesquite for a fire also. Joe had spent many nights here.

"Looks good. I'll ride back a short way to that rise and should be able to see the others coming." Fred stated.

"Ok. I'll get a fire laid and set out a picket line." Joe replied.

The campsite had been cleared some by others and Joe had never seen a snake around here. This was nice since no one wanted to give company to such. Joe worked away at setting a fire ring and getting wood for it. He pictured different places for bedrolls for the night. There was a small creek about 50 yards from the main camp and this would be great for the horses. He had things set fairly well when he heard the others coming. The squad rode in with Fred and the prisoners. The soldiers helped the prisoners dismount and made sure they were tied well yet. Next everyone unsaddled the horses and tossed their bedrolls on the ground.

One of the soldiers was said to be a good camp cook so he was nominated for the job. He set about immediately and started cooking beans on the fire. They had hardtack with them and Joe had managed to get some bacon to give good flavor to the beans. Things looked real good now. The horses were staked out so they could get some grass. They would be picketed for the night however. Army horses did not always stand around like Jean always did.

The darkness was closing in after everyone had eaten. Joe brought up some fresh canteens of water and they sat around the fire for a brief time. Finally it was time for bed. The prisoners were still tied and two men were to on guard during the night. The guards would change every three hours to give everyone the rest. Joe drifted into slumber land.

The next two days ran out fine and toward the end of the third day they could see Benson ahead. As they walked down the main street, they attracted some attention. The prisoners were a sight seldom seen like this. The guess by most townsmen was they were very bad men. Joe stopped at the marshal's office and checked in. He asked for cell space over the night. Benson was small and only had two jail cells. The prisoners would not in luxury for the night. After they were locked up, Joe and Fred walked to the café for supper. The Army personnel had already found a campsite at the edge of town. Joe had thanked them and advised he would buy them a beer if they could come to the saloon later. They all agreed to this with relish.

After supper, Joe and Fred got a hotel room from the only place in town. The train to Tucson arrived about 10 am.

"Suppose you wont be back around Bowie for a while now. You probably think everything is clear with your last work there." Fred told Joe.

"Well someone has to do the work. Don't see you bustin to get things going." Joe laughed.

"Well stop by whenever you are in the area and I might even buy you a drink." Fred remarked.

"Yup. The least you could do." Joe stated. "See you later." The two walked to their rooms for the night.

CHAPTER TWENTY-FOUR

T he next morning Joe and Fred met again for breakfast. The day was wonderful with its sun shining fully down on the small town. Fred had to hurry with his breakfast since the soldiers would be ready to head back to Bowie shortly. Joe had some time before 10 am to spend. They two ate and said their goodbyes. Joe walked to the train station and arranged for tickets to Tucson. There generally were not many people on this route. This train came from Bisbee and only went to Tucson.

Joe boarded the train just before 10 am and cuffed his prisoners to seats. They would ride to Tucson and then be held in that jail until the trial. The prisoners were pleased the horseback ride was done. Trains were much better for riding. The train lurched out of the town right after 10. It was about a three-hour ride to Tucson and the scenery was enjoyable as Joe rode along. There was only one other passenger on the car and he appeared to be a drummer. Joe was thinking he should have brought a bottle on board but the trip would not be very long. The prisoners were not very talkative during the ride and things were basically boring.

The train slowed into Tucson and stopped at the station. Joe had sent a telegram from Benson and asked the Sheriff for assistance at the station. He wanted at least one other man to assist in the walk to the jail. He stepped off the train with the prisoners and saw a deputy standing on the platform.

"Hello Sheriff. Glad to see you could help." Joe greeted.

"Got some bad ones?" The man answered.

"Probably not so bad but a few more than I cared to walk down the street with." Joe answered.

The two lawmen walked the prisoners to the jail and Joe signed them in.

"How's the new Sheriff doing?" Joe asked.

"Seems to be working in fine." The deputy stated.

"Well good. Be glad to buy you a drink over at the saloon across the street when you have time." Joe stated.

"Sounds great. Give me about ten minutes." The deputy answered.

"Met you over there." Joe answered as he walked out the door.

Joe walked across the street.

"HEY LAWMAN!" A loud voice yelled.

Joe looked around slowly and saw a man in the middle of the street looking at him. Joe did not recognize the man. He slowly turned toward the man, watching his hands closely.

"You the coward that brought the men in on the train?" The man asked.

"What's that to you?" Joe asked.

"You stinking law jerks are always grabbing someone for nothing." The man stated. "I think it's time you were finished."

Joe said nothing and stood squarely while watching the man carefully. The man was working his hands making fists on and off. This was a sign of a man not sure of his coming play. Seconds strung out like hours and Joe said nothing. He had seen men like this before and basically they were never very good at gunplay.

"Make you play lawman!" The man said loudly.

"You got no call for this. I don't want to kill you over nothing." Joe stated.

The man shifted his wait and moved one boot a little. He definitely was not good at this. Joe did not know what to do to stop the man.

"Why don't you step in the saloon with me and I'll buy you a beer." Joe asked.

"Fat chance chicken. You must be really scared of me by now." The man smirked.

"No, just hate to kill an idiot. Too much of that anymore." Joe stated.

The man stood looking at Joe and sweat was dripping from the man's forehead. The man kept working his hands and shifted his eyes from side to side. Joe could not think of anything to say to help stop this. Time was a friend to Joe however. The more time used the more the man might loose his nerve. He appeared to not have much now anyway.

The man wiped his right hand on his pants leg. He shifted his eyes again and seemed to be looking for someway to get out of this.

"Just let it drop man." Joe stated.

"The Hell I will!" The man stated as he grabbed for his sixgun.

The world stood still for a tenth of a second as Joe drew his pistol. The .45 spoke and the man in the street looked at Joe with a question in his eyes. He slowly looked down at his chest and saw a red dot appear. Slowly the ground rose to meet the man. He never saw anything else.

The deputy was running out of the office now.

"Sorry I didn't get out here sooner. I was in the back and didn't see things starting." The deputy stated.

"Guess the man was tired of living. He didn't take my offers to stop things." Joe stated.

"I'll get the undertaker. Then meet you in the saloon. Suppose you could use that now." The deputy said.

"Yeh, suppose so." Joe said as he turned to walk into the saloon.

"I saw everything Ranger. You gave him enough chances to stop things." The bartender stated as he set a bottle and glass in front of Joe. "Sure glad I didn't get into your business."

"Seldom like this but now and then things don't go well." Joe stated.

Joe downed four drinks rapidly. He then took the bottle to a table and sat down. The deputy came in shortly and sat down. The bartender brought him a glass.

"The undertaker is cleaning things up out there." The deputy stated.

The two men sat for another half hour then the deputy had to be on a patrol. Joe asked him about supper and they agreed to meet at the café down the street. Joe walked outside and headed toward the gunsmith here. He needed to restock his ammo and make sure he had plenty for the natives again. The gunsmith was talkative today and they discussed some of the new rifles that were coming out. There was a new bolt action one from England that was making the rounds. Joe still thought his Winchester lever action was better. He wanted guns that were reliable and reasonable in price.

Joe walked out again and went to get a room at the hotel close to the Sheriff's Office. He figured he could use a bath also. This would be good before supper. He had relaxed now from the gunplay and wondered about the coming trial for the prisoners. He hoped it didn't take too long. He wanted to get back to Tombstone and Huachuca. Old thoughts were returning to Joe. He had been getting more ideas of quitting this line of work. He just did not know what he would do then.

Joe got a bath and had his trail clothes taken out for cleaning. He walked outside again and headed for the saloon. He would meet the deputy for supper in a few minutes. He was looking for a good steak now and knew a couple of places that had such. The saloon was quiet yet and Joe had a couple of drinks then headed toward the café for his steak.

The deputy met him there and they discussed various things about the town. Things were about the same even without Sam. The deputy had information about the trial for the prisoners Joe brought in. The Judge had agreed to start things in the morning about 10 am. This was fine with Joe. He would send a telegraph to headquarters later and advise them of everything.

The two men ate and then greeted each other. Joe would meet later with the deputy if he were around. Right now he headed toward the hotel to rest a little. The day had been full and he was tired.

A WASTELAND OF OUTLAWS

CHAPTER TWENTY-FIVE

The next day came in cloudy. It really did not look like rain but a person never knew. Joe had breakfast and then walked to the stable to check on Jean. She was doing fine and the young lad was making sure she didn't need anything. He left the stable and walked the streets for a time. He was waiting for 10 to come around. Finally about 9:30 he went to the Sheriff's Office to help with the transfer of prisoners to the courtroom. At 10 sharp the Judge entered the court and things began. Joe was the only witness for the prosecutor. There were no defense witnesses. The entire trial lasted only 30 minutes. The Judge sentenced the men to 15 years in Yuma and dismissed the court.

Joe walked to the telegraph office and sent a wire to headquarters. He wanted to head out to Tombstone now and hoped they had nothing for him right now. He advised the telegrapher he would be at the saloon across from the Sheriff's Office. He walked into the saloon and found no one there. The bartender had just set out some lunch items so Joe made himself at home.

Joe ate his lunch and watched the street outside. There was little activity outside for this time of day. He hoped headquarters would be returning his wire soon. He spent an hour at the saloon, and then walked back outside. The street was basically empty yet. He walked back to the telegraph office to check for any messages. Just as he walked in, the telegrapher was finishing a message. He wrote everything out and handed it to Joe. Headquarters advised they had nothing for now and suggested Joe head back toward Tombstone. Joe felt relieved and very glad for everything.

He walked to the stable and saddled Jean. Then walked her to the hotel to check out of his room. He was ready to go in half an hour. He walked to the Sheriff's Office and advised them he was leaving. He was happy to be going now. The deputy invited him for a drink before going an Joe wanted to get a bottle for the road anyway. They spent about 30 minutes at the saloon and Joe told the deputy he needed to get on the trail. Joe walked out and mounted Jean heading out of town. He had a light heart now and felt very good.

Joe rode along and felt like a king of the Territory. He thought again about quitting but then he wondered what might be next. He knew friends and enjoyed Tombstone. His mind wandered as he rode and thoughts of the future were blurry. He figured to continue for now and see how fate might come. He knew he had made his mark in the Territory and felt good about his work. A man should be happy and proud of his work.